HE WANTS

ALISON MOORE
HE WANTS

BIBLIOASIS
WINDSOR, ONTARIO

FIRST EDITION

Library and Archives Canada Cataloguing in Publication

Moore, Alison, 1971-, author
    He wants / Alison Moore.

Originally published: London : Salt, [2014].
Issued in print and electronic formats.
ISBN 978-1-77196-056-4 (paperback).--ISBN 978-1-77196-057-1 (ebook)

    I. Title.

PR6113.O553H42 2016   823'.92   C2015-907266-2
                                              C2015-907267-0

Edited by Dan Wells
Copy-edited by Dan Wells
Typeset by Chris Andrechek
Cover Design by Gordon Robertson

PRINTED AND BOUND IN CANADA

For Ian and Kay

'We all experience within us . . . the desire to be transported from darkness into light, to be touched by the hand of that which is not of this world.'

NICK CAVE, *The Secret Life of the Love Song*

'We are meant to be hungry.'

LIONEL SHRIVER, *Big Brother*

WHAT DO YOU WANT?

THE FRONT DOOR is mostly glass, a pane as tall and wide as a man. In town, at night, the shopfront windows are protected with steel mesh screens and metal shutters. Even the churches have grilles over the stained glass windows. This café is not in the town, though; it is in the village and the owner has nothing like that, just a lock on the wooden frame of this single-glazed door. It is not night-time anyway; it is broad daylight, mid-morning. The door frame is painted yellow, a warm, bright yellow like sunshine or pollen.

There is a handmade sign hanging on the door, behind the glass. It says, 'WELCOME', but the lettering is small and the greeting appears tentative. It is the sort of sign that is hung with string and could be flipped around when your welcome was withdrawn.

Underneath it, there is another, larger one saying, 'NO DOGS'. It is not the sort that can be turned to say something different; it is stuck to the glass.

Sydney ties his dog's lead to a drainpipe. The dog settles down on the slabs, sighing through her nostrils as she watches Sydney walk away.

Inside the café, only one of the tables is occupied, by a young woman breastfeeding a baby. Sydney slips off the rucksack he is carrying, pulls out a chair and sits down opposite her. 'Hello,' he says, smiling, showing his teeth. 'You're Ruth.'

He has disturbed the baby, who is twisting around now, looking for the source of the deep voice, while the mother struggles to get the baby feeding again, her milk wasting.

'No,' she says. 'I'm not.'

Sydney regards her while he considers this, and then excuses himself. He scrapes back his chair and stands, looking around. He is ravenous, his stomach growling like something at the zoo waiting to be thrown some meat. He wants a McDonald's, or an all-you-can-eat buffet, but instead he is here. There is salad behind glass on the far side of the room.

He wanders over to the counter. Looking towards a doorway at the back of the café, he calls out, 'Hello?' The doorway is hung with a curtain of thin plastic strips. No one comes through. Sydney waits, looking at the plated salads, the mottled bananas, the Death by chocolate on the blackboard. 'Hello?'

he calls again. A radio is on behind the curtain. He can hear adverts, the jingles of a local station. He has begun to move towards the hatch via which he could get behind the counter, when through the curtain comes a man in a floral apron, his arms opening wide for Sydney, his smile broad, although there is anxiety in the straining of the skin around his eyes. He says to Sydney, 'So, you're back, are you?' Lowering his arms again, he leans his weight on the counter between them. 'It's changed a bit around here since you last saw it, eh?'

'Not that much,' says Sydney, removing his coat.

The man's gaze travels from the thinness of Sydney's silver-stubbled face down to the leanness of the body emerging from the shabby, gabardine coat. 'Are you hungry?' He waves a hand towards the fridge and says, 'What do you want?'

'I don't want salad,' says Sydney. 'I need a bowl of water for the dog.'

'You've got a new dog?'

'It's my old dog's puppy,' says Sydney. 'She's old herself now though. A friend of mine's been looking after her while I've been away.'

The man finds an empty ice cream tub and fills it with cold tap water. 'I'll take this out to her,' he says. 'You have a think about what you want.'

Sydney wanders back over to where the mother still sits with her baby, who is latched on again. Sitting down at an adjacent table, Sydney stretches out his long legs until his feet are underneath the woman's table. 'You're not Ruth?' he says.

'I'm not Ruth,' she says, without looking up.

The man in the apron, having taken the water out to the dog, stops on his way back to the counter to take the woman's empty coffee cup away.

'I'll have another cup of coffee, please,' she says.

'I'll get this one,' says Sydney, putting his hand into his pocket and pulling out a pound note. The man raises an eyebrow at Sydney, who at that moment feels like a child trying to buy something with toy money. Shaking his head, the man goes off to fetch the coffee, leaving Sydney to put away his redundant bank note. Sydney turns to the woman. 'My name's Sydney,' he says, 'with a "y", like the capital of Australia.'

'Sydney's not the capital of Australia,' she says.

Sydney sits back, withdrawing his limbs, his foot knocking against the leg of her table. The baby jerks its head back and the mother winces.

The man returns with the woman's cup of coffee. Looking at Sydney's trainers, and at his rucksack, onto which the flags of various countries have been sewn, he says to Sydney, 'You look like you're ready for a quick getaway. Are you off somewhere?'

'Not today,' says Sydney. 'I'm meeting someone here.'

'Who are you meeting?' asks the man.

'A lady called Ruth.'

'You're meeting her here?' The man, glancing at the little plastic clock on the wall, says, 'Barry Bolton will be here soon.'

Sydney reaches instantly for his coat.

'Owe him money?' asks the man, regarding Sydney with concern.

Sydney doesn't reply but he is pushing back his chair, getting to his feet. He puts on his coat, picks up his rucksack and moves towards the door. As he ducks out, the bell over the door jangles like a town crier's handbell and the 'welcome' sign swings as the door closes behind him.

The debt is decades old. He has no idea now of its size.

When the dog sees Sydney coming out of the café, she begins to whine for him. Sydney releases her from the drainpipe and hurries the short distance to a row of new cottages, slipping into the front garden of one. He does not know who lives here. He positions himself inside an open porch, peering at the nearby cars, which are all parked and empty. He does not know what Ruth's car looks like but she does not seem to be here yet. He turns his head in the opposite direction and sees Barry Bolton walking down the hill, coming from the butcher's towards the café. Sydney puts his hand to his chest, feeling a twinge in his heart.

Barry is a big man, although his feet are small enough that he can wear his mother's shoes. He avoids stepping, with his little feet, on the cracks between the paving stones. Reaching the café, he goes inside. In less than a minute, he is out again, holding an envelope. He crosses the road and sits down on a bench in the middle of the village green, across from the café. Planting his small feet wide, he opens the envelope, takes out a wad of bank notes and counts them. When he has counted them twice, he puts them back in the envelope and tucks it into an inside pocket of his coat. He continues to sit, though. He looks like a man who is waiting for something.

Sydney, loitering in the porch, wishes that the day was not so bright, that he was not so exposed. He would prefer shadow. He looks at his watch, wondering how long he will have to stay there, hiding like some scallywag.

There is a sign in the living-room window, advertising a vacant bed. 'Bedroom to let', it says. Sydney wonders whether anyone ever answers the advert, whether anyone ever comes to this quiet village to occupy that spare bed. Should the owner of the house come to the door and discover him standing in the porch, Sydney will ask about the room; he will express an interest in the bed.

It is chilly. He is seizing up from the cold and from standing for so long. The dog is lying on her belly again, on the porch's stone tiles. Sydney, slowly, stiffly, joins her down there, lowering his thin backside to the ground. The dog gazes at him with her big, brown eyes. It looks like love but she barely knows him. He only recently picked her up from his friend, the friend with whom he had left his dog before going away. Technically, this is not his dog. Really, this offspring of his dog belongs to his friend, but this friend, having taken receipt of a dog, felt that a dog—rather than an empty dog collar, an empty dog bowl, an empty dog bed—is what needed to be returned to Sydney in due course. This friend knows Barry Bolton too and has perhaps learnt to avoid having debts. Sydney wonders if the dog is missing the friend who was, until this morning, her owner, or whether all she really wants is to know where her next meal is coming from.

When Sydney hears the door opening behind him, a part of him anticipates his mother coming to scold him, as she did when he was a boy and dared to sit on hard curbs and cold walls; he half-expects to hear her yelling, 'Do you want piles?'

He turns to see a man of his own age standing in the doorway, staring down at him.

'I'm here about the room,' says Sydney.

'I didn't hear you knock,' says the man. He looks at Sydney's dog. 'No dogs,' he says.

Sydney's knees crack as he gets to his feet, and the dog sighs.

The man leads Sydney down the hallway. Coming to a stop before the stairs, he says, 'You'll have your breakfast in the dining room.' He opens the nearest door and Sydney sees a chintzy dining table set for breakfast even though it is not breakfast time, as if, like Miss Havisham, the man just keeps it that way all the time.

'What do you like for breakfast?' asks the man. 'I can offer you Sugar Puffs, Coco Pops, Chocolatey Cheerios, Golden Nuggets, Golden Puffs and Honey Wows.'

'All I really want is a fag,' says Sydney, 'first thing.'

'Oh,' says the man, closing the door of the breakfast room.

They climb the stairs, and when they get to the top, the man opens a door and shows Sydney into a front bedroom. Sydney thinks at first that he has been shown the wrong room because this is a child's bedroom, a young teen's bedroom, with an astronaut on the single duvet, but the man says, 'Everything's clean. The drawers and the wardrobe have been emptied for now, so there'll be space for your things, but I don't want to change too much in here in case Martin comes back. If he came back and wanted his room, I'd need to ask you to leave. You'd get your deposit back.'

Sydney nods and goes to the window, looking out at the village green, at Barry who is still on the bench.

'It's cold out,' says the man, 'but that radiator's on.'

Sydney, standing warming his legs, asks the man about the rent. He keeps him talking about the bills and the cost of living, but still Barry does not move away, and in the end Sydney has to say to the man, 'Is there a back garden?' The man looks delighted.

He takes Sydney out through the back door, next to which, on the patio, there is a rabbit hutch with a young rabbit inside. The hutch looks brand new. 'Martin's always wanted a pet,' says the man.

He indicates an empty flower bed at the near end of the garden. 'Sweet peas,' he says. 'They're his favourite.'

'It's not the right time of year for planting sweet peas,' says Sydney.

'I put them in last spring.'

'Well, if they've not come through yet,' says Sydney, 'I don't think they're going to.'

The man gazes down at the cold soil as if watching it. 'We'll see,' he says.

They make their way down an increasingly muddy path to the vegetable patch in which the man has planted rhubarb. 'Martin loves rhubarb,' he says, surveying this plot in which, by March, he should have six square feet of the stuff.

'If you don't mind,' says Sydney, 'I'll leave through your back gate.'

'Oh,' says the man. 'Of course.' He walks with Sydney to the gate, where he jots down his phone number and hands it over. 'Call me,' he says to Sydney, who will not.

The gate brings Sydney into an alley. He walks down to the far end, coming out well away from the house and the village green, and then he remembers his dog, which is still waiting outside the man's front door. He can't walk up the street to the front of the house because Barry will see him. He turns around and goes back down the alley, retracing his steps. When he arrives at the man's gate, he peers over it, scanning the garden, the patio, the rear of the house. The man is not there. Sydney leans over and lifts the catch, letting himself into the garden. He walks up the muddy path, in between the well-tended plots, watching the back windows. The man is not in sight. Only the rabbit in the hutch is watching him. He could knock, but it would be a whole lot easier to just get in and out without having to explain himself, without being noticed. He can see—through the patterned glass in the back door—that the kitchen is empty. He tries the handle. Finding the door unlocked, he goes inside, back into the warm house. The man's boots, muddy from the garden, are on the doormat. The kettle is boiling beside a clean cup, inside which a dry teabag, a shiny teaspoon and the tiny white dot of a sweetener are ready, waiting for the hot water. Sydney stands still for a moment and listens but hears no sounds from inside the house. He steps into the hallway, making his way past the closed dining-room door and down to the far end where he quietly opens the front door. The dog looks up, wags her tail and gets to her feet. Sydney brings her into the house and closes the door again, but the closing is louder than the opening. He can hear the man moving around upstairs now, in the front bedroom. He hears the man call out, 'Hello?' and after a pause, 'Martin, is that you?'

Sydney leads his dog back down the hallway, through the kitchen and out of the back door, which he closes behind him, leaving a trail of mud from his boots all along the hallway carpet for the man to find and puzzle over.

HE DOES NOT
WANT SOUP

'YOU DON'T WANT anything, do you, Dad?' says Ruth, on her way out of the living room. Lewis opens his mouth to reply, but he can't decide whether he does or not, he can't say what he might want, so he doesn't say anything.

Ruth takes their teacups through to the kitchen, puts them heavily into the sink and turns on the tap.

It is still close enough to winter to be dark outside at getting-up time. Ruth complains about having to drag herself out of her warm bed at what feels like four o'clock in the morning, but Lewis rather likes how it feels to wash his face in the bathroom sink before it is light. It makes him feel like a man with a job to do, like a farmer rising before dawn, like a jet-setter with an early flight to catch.

It is dark, still, when Ruth drops her boy off at his new nursery. She has said to Lewis that it must seem to the boy as if she is leaving him with strangers in the middle of the night. 'Yes,' said Lewis, 'it probably does.'

By the time she gets to Lewis's house, though, it is almost light.

Sitting in his armchair in front of the television, Lewis can see her standing looking out of the kitchen window while she waits for the water to run warm, her fingertips in the cold drizzle. The snowdrops are still out and the daffodils should soon be through. She raises her voice to say to him, 'Your lawn's looking a bit dead.' He once pointed out an azalea that had turned bright red—not just its flowers but its leaves as well were all scarlet, glorious, and Ruth told him it was dying. You got a final show, she said, this burst of beauty before it expired. He'd had an oleander, too, of which he was rather fond, but she took one look and said it was poisonous and that it had to go. She would not let the boy play in Lewis's garden until the plant had gone, and even now she will not let the boy go in there, because if some toxic part of it is still lying around he will put it in his mouth.

Whenever Ruth glances at Lewis's garden, he holds his breath, wondering what's coming, what will have to go.

She washes out the cups and then stands in the kitchen doorway, drying her hands on a tea towel while she tells him about the course she is thinking of taking. 'I am going to do one this year,' she says. For years, she has been planning on doing a degree, trying to decide on one: French, with German or Italian or Spanish, with a year abroad, perhaps in Paris; or French with Chinese, a year in China; or French with European Studies or Global Studies or Philosophy, or Modern Languages with History of Art. Now that she has the boy she has been looking into evening classes instead, languages without the year abroad. She goes back into the kitchen to hang the damp tea towel over the cold radiator.

'What about the boy?' calls Lewis. 'I can look after him.'

'John will look after him,' she says.

Yes, thinks Lewis, John will look after him. John is a good man, a good father, and hospitable to Lewis, even though Lewis cannot bear, now, to be in a room with him.

Lewis has sometimes thought about retaking his maths A level, in which he had got such a disappointing grade. He does not know where his old textbooks are though. He does not want to have to buy them all over again. He says to Ruth, 'Do you know where my old maths books are?'

'No,' she says. 'What maths books? You don't mean your old school books? What do you want them for? It's all done differently now, you know. Everything's changed since your day.' She wanders over to the bookshelves. 'You're always losing your books.'

He has only recently noticed just how many Bliss Tempest novels Edie managed to accumulate. They were just about all she read, and she read them repeatedly. She read them in bed; he would switch off his lamp and she would still be reading. There was always one on her bedside table. He has been finding them all over the house, in fact. He has been collecting them up and putting them back onto his wife's shelf in the living room. She probably has the writer's entire oeuvre. Some of them, she once told him, were out of print and could only be got from second-hand bookshops or private collectors. 'They might be worth something one day,' she said. The men in them always reminded her of Lewis. She mentioned this to him and he was amused to imagine himself as a character in a romance because he did not think of himself as a romantic man. He himself has never read these well-thumbed books of Edie's. His books are on the shelves above—his literature, along with his father's, the bibles and reference books.

Despite his efforts, though, despite the returning of all these books to the shelves, there are still gaps where there should not be gaps, spaces at which he stares, wondering what is missing, becoming anxious about books that might have been borrowed and might never be returned.

Edie used to drive the book mobile to the villages, scattering books, it seemed to Lewis, far and wide, driving off leaving them strewn, like the books she sometimes left behind in hotel rooms or on the roof of their car as they drove away. She claimed not to do this, but she did; the books went missing.

Lewis remembers how the library tipped very slightly towards you as you entered, when you put your weight on the steps, and how it swayed underfoot while you were browsing. In the book mobile, the librarian still stamps the book's paper insert, printing the date in black or purple ink, just like in real libraries in the sixties. In the town library now, you don't take your books to the lady behind the desk, you put your books into an opening in a big, black machine that scans them. You can leave without speaking to a soul.

When Edie retired, she missed driving the book mobile, doing her rounds, seeing the countryside, and so Lewis, who had not been to the smaller villages for a very long time, drove her out there. He remembers pointing out some cows he saw galloping across a field. 'Cows don't gallop,' said Edie, who had not noticed them. But Lewis had seen them; he had seen them galloping through the thick grass. He loved driving through the countryside and the villages, slowing for horses, pausing to admire some particularly attractive cottage, coming to a stop outside the only house in a terrace that was not plastered and painted or clad, its bare bricks giving it an exposed and vulnerable appearance. Later, he went back on his own, although he found the drive lonely without Edie. Coming to a stop outside that unclad house, he sat gazing towards it, his engine idling. He eyed the fine yellow car parked in the street at the front, and peered down the side of the house towards the back door, which was ajar. He saw the grey head of a man bent forward in the garden, working his way along the borders. He could not see the man's face. Lewis wound down his window, his engine still running. The man, slowly standing, a few dead plants hanging from his hands, looked out towards the street and, through narrowed eyes, saw Lewis. 'He isn't here,' shouted the man. Or he would see Lewis from the front window and come to the front door to shout across the road, 'He isn't here. He doesn't live here.'

Lewis no longer drives. Ruth is relieved. She always expected something to happen to him. She gave him a cellular phone, just in case he got into trouble, but he never needed to use it. He drove for more than fifty years without having an accident, except for one incident in a rental car. He took it back expecting to have a row, to have to pay through the nose. It would be on the bank statement, he thought, for Edie to see and query. He would have to admit to carelessness, dangerous driving, reckless behaviour. The man at the rental company did not raise an eyebrow though. He said it was nothing, just a scratch, and did not even charge him; he just let him walk away. In the end, Lewis stopped driving because of his painful knee. He keeps the cellular phone in a drawer in the kitchen.

'I doubt you realise what you've lost anyway,' says Ruth, looking at his bookshelves. 'You never remember what you've read.'

It is true. There are books he's had for decades that he thought he'd never got round to opening, and then when he did finally read them, he remembered, as he neared the end, that he had in fact read this before; or he found his own pencilled notes in the margins, perhaps a hundred pages in.

'I've put some soup in the fridge for your lunch,' says Ruth. 'Are you going to get dressed? Maybe go out and get some fresh air later? You haven't been out of the house all week.'

'I've been to the bin,' says Lewis. (He stood at his boundary, with one hand on the lid of his garbage bin. It has the number of his house painted on it, so that it will not get lost. The zero is a foot across. He watched a plane go overhead.)

Ruth is in the hallway now, putting on her coat before coming back for a kiss. He never knows what part of him she's aiming for. She kisses the edge of his ear, his hair. 'I'm off now,' she says.

'All right,' he says.

She has to slam the door behind her because it won't close properly otherwise. When Lewis hears the bang, the rattle of the letterbox, he stands and makes his way to the front room. He watches through the window, through the net curtain, as she walks to the gate. When he sees that her car is parked out there, he is surprised. Her house is only down the road and the office where she works is just a bit further on. She always walks; she never does the journey by car.

Getting in behind the wheel, she puts her soup bag down on the passenger seat, straps herself in and drives away without looking back at the house. She keeps Susan Boyle in the CD player. She likes 'I Dreamed a Dream'. She sings along.

He notices, too, that she is not driving towards the office. She seemed, he thinks, to be in a bit of a rush. He wonders where she is going, what errand she might be running in her little car. And was she wearing a new coat?

He looks at the stone lion standing in concrete at the far end of the path, its head turned towards him, facing the house. It ought really to be watching the gate. They usually come in pairs, he thinks, these guardians of gateways. He only got the one. Ruth used to love that lion. Her pushchair always had to be stopped beside it so that she could reach out and pet its hard head, run her hand over the cold furrows of its brow. There is a layer of lichen on the stone now. It is powdery to the touch.

When Ruth is no longer in sight, Lewis turns away. He goes back into the living room and switches off the television before heading to the kitchen to look at his lawn from the window. He does not think it is dying, except perhaps in certain places where it has been used as a toilet by the neighbourhood's cats. He should get a dog to keep these intruders at bay. He used to have one, but it got out and was lost, perhaps to the traffic and the council's waste department, or perhaps it found someone who gave it nicer dog food.

Edie did not much like dogs. She got a kitten, a scrap of a thing that came and went from Lewis's lap without him noticing. He let it out of the house too soon and they never saw it again.

He opens up the fridge to take a look at what Ruth has left him. She comes every morning, on her way to work. She does administrative work for an arts organisation that has no theatre, no art gallery, not even a café; it is just an office and he does not really know what she does there. Whatever it is, she has been doing it for twenty years. She comes here—letting herself in with her own door key—at the same time every morning. She makes him a cup of her milky tea and leaves a Tupperware tub of soup in the fridge for his dinner. She makes these soups herself, with leftovers, all the vegetables her little boy won't eat. The soups are grey-brown, the same colour as Ruth's hair.

There is not much else in the fridge. There is a supermarket in the village, on Small Street, just past the secondary school. It is a perfectly good supermarket and within walking distance but he does not go there. When he was still driving, he once parked for more than the permitted two hours in the parking lot of this supermarket. A few weeks later, he received a letter stamped with the scales of justice, citing video evidence of his infringement of the rules and fining him heavily, under threat of court. He paid the fine but has not been back to the store since, even though it is the only one that he can get to now. Ruth thinks he is staging a boycott, being stubborn, but really he is just too embarrassed to return to the scene of the crime.

What Lewis really wants is one of Edie's steak and kidney puddings, her chicken curry, her hotpot. He wants that excellent beef Wellington he had in a restaurant once. He does not remember what restaurant it was, somewhere on a summer holiday perhaps. It was a long time ago. He does not want soup but Ruth brings it anyway and Lewis eats it. He hates to waste it, and hates to see her taking away, with the slightest of comments, his tub of uneaten soup. More often than not he eats it cold, straight from the fridge, minutes before she arrives to take away the empty tub and leave him with another. He prefers pizza. He has discovered the joys of pizza delivery services. He orders Supremes and Delights and they are brought to his door by young men on motorbikes.

He once wondered about getting a motorbike.

Closing the fridge, he looks at the calendar on the wall beside it. Every square is blank except for one, and that one, he realises, looking at the day, at the date, is today. It says: *3 pm*. But what, he wonders, is happening today at 3 pm? What else was he supposed to write before he got distracted, by a thought or the doorbell or a cat scratching in the garden? He has no idea if someone is coming or if he is supposed to be somewhere. No one ever comes except for Ruth, and there is nowhere he goes to other than the nursing home and the church on Sundays, and the pub, sometimes, for a shandy and a speciality sausage. He feels a flutter of excitement in his stomach at the thought that something out of the ordinary might be going to happen to him today.

WHEN HE WAS A CHILD, HE WANTED TO GO TO THE MOON

IN A PHOTOGRAPH on his living-room mantelpiece, Lewis is four years old and riding his mother's tea tray down an icy slope with an almighty grin on his face. He imagines his nose and cheeks pinked by the cold air, although the camera has made them grey. It makes Ruth anxious, this picture; it worries her to see him hurtling down, as if he might still come to harm at the end of the slope, as if he could still break his bones.

Ruth was always a nervous girl, scared of many things—climbing a jungle gym in a park, climbing the ladder of a bunk bed, riding a bicycle or being on roller skates, being alone in the dark. Lewis could not stand it, that she did not have guts. He wanted a fearless child. Instead he had a girl who always wanted her mother. He wanted a boy, but he and Edie had left it too late and only had the one child. Perhaps nowadays it would be different, there would be things they could do; they store embryos in freezers, although some fail to survive the freezing, or they explode when thawed. He thinks of Walt Disney, cryonically frozen, to be thawed out in a distant future, although apparently this never happened.

When Lewis was a child, he liked to climb. He got up trees. He imagined being able to jump from up there, to spread his arms and will himself to fly. Instead, up in the branches, he read his comics and books: *The Brave Book for Boys* and *The Schoolboy's Annual: Tales of Sport and Adventure*—hard-covered hand-me-downs, one bright yellow and one with bombers on the front. Lewis, whose name meant 'famous warrior', wanted to be the boys in these stories, to have their adventures at sea and up mountains, their encounters with smugglers and bears, their golden age of boyhood; he wanted to at least have their dogs. Above all, the character he most wanted to be was Flash Gordon. He wanted to have Flash Gordon's bravado and Flash Gordon's torso, to travel in a rocket ship, to travel in a starship that was faster than light.

His mother did not like him being up in trees. She worried that he would get stuck up there in a storm and then he might get hit by lightning. He never was up a tree, though, during a storm. Once or twice, he was outside when he heard thunder, and he stood still, holding his breath, but he never did get struck by a bolt of high voltage electricity.

They lived in a different part of the village then. They lived on Small Street, near the secondary school. He can see the very spot from the back bedroom of the house he lives in now. For a time, in this house on Small Street, they lived next door to relatives—his father's uncle, who moved away when Lewis was young, and his father's cousin, whom Lewis does not even remember.

Lewis's back bedroom window is also where he and Edie had stood watching for the Perseid meteor shower. He had thrown the window open to let the night air in, imagining explosions like fireworks. The trails of light were infrequent, though, and hard, in fact, to see at all, and silent. Edie referred to them later, to Ruth, as shooting stars, but they were not stars, as Lewis had been disappointed to discover; they were particles like dust, burning up in Earth's atmosphere. The comet from which the particles came was long gone and would not be back for something like a hundred and fifteen years. Lewis wonders if Ruth's boy will live to see it. Probably not, he thinks.

Lewis has always lived near the countryside. Even when he went away to university and might have gone to a city, he went instead to a plate glass university on the edge of a town, surrounded by countryside. Decades later, hearing stories about this university's liberalism and radicalism, Lewis's father eyed him suspiciously, wondering what he'd been doing down there—he used the word 'hotbed'—and Lewis had to say, 'It wasn't like that when I was there.' It's a city now, apparently, although he hasn't been back.

The best countryside around here is out near the smaller villages, the smallest of which is known by its prefix, 'Nether'. His father took him rambling, looking for 'God's wonders', warning him about adders and hemlock. They picked great bunches of wild flowers and captured insects and small mammals in jars with tiny holes punched through the lid.

Lewis took eggs, once, from a bird's nest, from the nest of the handsome yellow bunting, the yellowhammer. He loved the brightness of the yellow on the throat and belly of the male; the female was duller. The yellow was brightest of all in the older males. He had one of the eggs in his pocket and one in each hand when his father saw what he was up to and told him to put them back. And Lewis did put them back, even the one he had in his pocket, but as they walked on, his father said to him, 'The mother will probably reject them now.' Lewis, lying in bed that night, worried about these eggs and whether they really would be rejected by the mother bird, even though he had only touched them.

At school, there was an art teacher who walked around the dinner hall saying to one pupil, 'Your mother loves you,' and to another, 'Your mother doesn't love you,' as if he alone knew, or as if, by saying it, he made it so. Either way, if he came to a stop behind you, leaned over your red-jumpered shoulder and said, 'Your mother doesn't love you,' as he did one day to Lewis, who had until that moment been loved, you knew suddenly, certainly, with disappointment, in silent agony with your mouth still full of tomato-damp sandwich, that it was true, that something you had done, or something about you, had negated that vital love.

You don't see yellow buntings these days. What he remembers of the yellow bunting, aside from its yellow underparts and the abandoned eggs, are his father's demonstrations of the bird's song. 'Tit, tit, tit, tit, tit, tit, *tee*,' he chanted as they walked along, 'tit, tit, tit, tit, tit, tit, *tee*.' Lewis, staring at the ground, concentrating on snakes, found it alarming. Years later, when Lewis was eighteen or nineteen, he saw his father with *The Trial of Lady Chatterley* in his hands, breaking the book open and reading aloud, 'The word "fuck" or "fucking" occurs no less than thirty times. I have added them up . . . "Cunt" fourteen times; "balls" thirteen times; "shit" and "arse" six times apiece.' The unsettling effect of witnessing this language coming from his father's mouth was much the same as hearing his attempt at the yellow bunting's song.

They would come home from their rambles and cover the kitchen table with fistfuls of wilting wild flowers and jars containing creatures that Lewis always hoped—when they looked through his father's books—would prove to be something rare, but he was always disappointed. They once caught a snake but it was only a grass snake. He wanted to go to the jungle. He wanted to travel to the North Pole. He wanted to fly to the moon. (He wanted, really, to visit the sun but that was further away, and if you made it that far you'd get burnt and you'd never come back.)

Lewis grew up to become an Religious Studies teacher at the local secondary school, the same school he had attended as a boy and at which his father taught English. (The art teacher was still there, and Lewis saw him in the dinner hall saying to the pupils who had brown-bread sandwiches, 'Your mother loves you,' and to those with white-bread sandwiches, 'Your mother doesn't love you.') Lewis and his father, each a Mr Sullivan, were often confused in paperwork, 'Mr Sullivan' being taken to mean his father, Lawrence. In later decades, when Lawrence was no longer teaching there, Lewis ceased to be a Mr Sullivan at all and instead the children called him by his first name as if he were one of them. He had never liked being Lewis Sullivan because of the way the consonants ran together in the middle so that his edges disappeared.

As a young man, Lewis, daydreaming about his future, had pictured himself visiting his elderly mother in a bungalow. He imagined doing her shopping for her, putting up shelves, fetching things down from her loft. Instead, as it turned out, it was his father who remained in old age, whose shopping Lewis did and whose shelves Lewis put up, whose roof Lewis still lived under. On a few occasions, Lewis brought a male colleague—the art teacher, the chemistry teacher, a physical fitness instructor—round for dinner, but Lawrence was not the best host. 'Don't they have wives?' he would say of these men. 'Don't any of them have wives to get home to?'

When the school recruited a new librarian who was a single lady of Lewis's age, Lewis became a big reader of whatever classics the library carried. As he returned each of these books at the end of the loan period, he attempted to discuss them with her, but each time, Edie, eyeing the Austen, the Eliot, the Woolf, would say, 'I haven't read it. It's not my sort of thing.'

On their first date, they did not talk about books; they talked about food, what they had or had not eaten in their lives. 'I've never had beef Wellington,' said Edie. 'I've never had blood pudding,' said Lewis.

When Lewis and Edie had been courting for a year, Lewis's father asked if he planned to marry Edie. He asked again, many times, over the years, saying to Lewis, 'What are you waiting for?' They had been a couple for seven years before Lewis finally got around to proposing. After a three-year engagement, they married in the summer of 1977.

On his wedding day, Lewis was driven to the church by Edie's brother, who was his best man. En route, in a quiet side road still hung with decorations from the silver jubilee, they came across an old, yellow car that had come to a stop, its hazard lights flashing. 'We'd better go around it,' said Lewis. As they drew alongside it, Lewis noticed the hula girl on the dashboard, ready to dance but still for now. The driver was sitting on the hood, reclining against the windshield, sunbathing with his long legs out in front of him, one knee raised up. He had his shirt off. There was music coming from the car's stereo and the man was drumming his hands against the hood while the bunting fluttered above him, like someone on a float at a parade. They paused at the junction, and Edie's brother, glancing in the rearview mirror, said that they ought to go back and see if they could help. Lewis was looking in his wing mirror. 'We haven't got time to go back,' he said. 'I don't want to get my suit dirty. He looks like he's waiting for someone.' He opened his mouth to say something else, to say, 'I don't know,' but Edie's brother was already pulling out of the junction, pressing on in the direction of the church.

At the wedding, Edie's brother made a joke in his best man's speech about this half-naked man atop a broken-down car, and Lewis and Edie slow-danced to 'Everything I Own', a song that was forever afterwards on the radio, someone new recording it every few years. Lewis never mentioned to Edie that it was not really the romantic song she thought it was but a tribute to the songwriter's dead father, a love song for an old man.

When their baby came along, she was a biter. Edie bit the baby right back to teach her not to do it, but when the baby bit Lewis he just looked pained and that made Ruth laugh, displaying her sharp little teeth. 'You must bite her,' said Edie, but he could not bring himself to do it, and soon the moment had passed, it seemed to him, although Edie came over and bit her anyway. The baby screamed, and she screamed in the night, wanting Edie, who sometimes went to her and sometimes did not. (Lewis, conversely, had become quiet in bed. Every Friday, he put a pillow in between their headboard and the partition wall, and came without making a sound.)

When Ruth reached the age at which some little girls want to marry their fathers, she chose her grandfather, although he did not like the game. When she told Lawrence that she wanted to marry him, he ignored her, or he found some reason to leave the room.

In her teens, Ruth seemed interested only in pop stars and film stars who were either very old or dead. She never seemed to have a real boyfriend. One summer, during a family holiday at Butlins, she developed a crush on the ageing cabaret star. When they got home, she ran away, heading back to Bognor Regis to be with him. She was home again a week later and never mentioned him again. When, in her thirties, she married John, Lewis thought it might be a similar whim and has been waiting for it to pass, even though she was pregnant not long afterwards and that was years ago. Lewis does not find it easy to accept their dinner invitations but he adores the child. He had been expecting another girl, but it turned out to be a boy, the boy that he and Edie never had.

Lewis has tried to give the boy what his own father gave to him. He has attempted rambles. The boy walks along holding on to his toy binoculars through which one can look and see everything far less clearly than before. Like Ruth, though, the boy is anxious. Hoping to toughen him up, Lewis has instead given the boy a fear of bulls. Trying to capture a newt in a jar, Lewis trod on the creature, bursting its bright yellow belly, while the boy stood watching. To teach him how to climb a tree, Lewis helped the boy into the lower branches of one, and then got them both up onto the next branch and then the next, lifting and climbing, lifting and climbing, branch by branch without stopping to look down, until they were just about as high as they could go and they perched there, feeling proud of themselves, watching the insects that crawled along the ridges and valleys of the bark. It was only when the boy said that he wanted to get down again and Lewis had to contemplate the descent, that he realised the difficulty of it, of getting both himself and the boy safely down to the ground. He kept them up there for as long as he could before painstakingly bringing the boy down, scraping the skin from his limbs and afraid, the whole time, of plummeting. Like Ruth, the boy has a poor sense of balance. 'Did you not think,' said Ruth, later, inspecting the boy's wounds, his sprained ankle, 'about what you would do when you got up there? Did you think you could just stay there, the two of you, all night, or for ever?' When the boy hurts himself, he cries as if he might never stop. On another occasion, when Lewis returned the boy to his mother with a toenail split down the middle, Ruth said to Lewis, as if he knew nothing about children, as if he had none of his own, 'Children his age have a fear of being damaged.'

'He's only three,' said Lewis. 'He won't remember this.'

The shortness of the boy's memory is astonishing. His mother asks him if he wants to go to Pizza Hut for lunch, and he says yes, so she tells him they will all go to Pizza Hut for lunch. She puts on the boy's coat so that, she says, he will be warm on the way to Pizza Hut. They leave the house and get into the car so that, she tells him, they can drive to Pizza Hut. When they have been driving for a minute or two, he turns to his mother and asks her, 'Where are we going?'

When the broken toenail lifted after a few weeks, the skin underneath looked unsettlingly vulnerable. The new nail grew back a long time ago but the boy still mentions it.

The boy is now almost the same age as Lewis is in the photograph on the mantelpiece. 'I'll take him sledding,' thinks Lewis. 'When it snows I'll take him sledding on a tea tray.'

Also on the mantelpiece are a handful of birthday cards—one from Miranda, one from his father that says 'Joy', one from Ruth that says, 'You're 70!' It reminds him of Danny DeVito in *Throw Momma from the Train* shouting to his mother, 'You're alive!' It reminds him of those messages that are placed by the bedsides of people with memory loss: 'It's Tuesday. Your name is Lewis.' He has always been a Lewis. There has only ever been one person who called him Lewie, or Louie, as this person wrote it, filling him with vowels.

HE WANTS TO FLY

WHEN LEWIS WAS eighteen years old, his father took him to see Billy Graham. Lewis thought at first that they were going to America, that they would fly above the clouds, like Icarus. They would fly west, through half a dozen time zones, and having reached adulthood in England, where Lewis could legally buy beer, he would find that he was underage again. He imagined Florida and the Sun Belt and felt warm just thinking about being there. He imagined himself wearing shorts on a beach.

This did not happen though. His father was not taking him to America but up to Manchester, where Billy Graham was appearing at Maine Road football stadium. In the week before they went, his father talked ceaselessly about this man they would see, and it was clear to Lewis that they would not only see but *experience* him. Lewis's mother got fed up of hearing about it, but Lewis did not. He stayed close to his father, alert to any mention of Billy Graham and the imminent trip to Manchester. His father fairly hummed with anticipation; it radiated from him like heat, exciting Lewis too.

On the day of their journey, settling into their seats on the bus, his father said, 'You can feel the buzz,' and when he had said it a few times, Lewis almost could.

The bus driver, wearing a short-sleeved white shirt, a dark tie and sunglasses, made an announcement from the front of the bus. 'Ladies and gentlemen, we'll be taking off in a few minutes. I hope you enjoy travelling with us today,' he said, as if what he really wanted was to be an airline pilot, as if he might also tell them, as they travelled, what their cruising speed was and what the weather was like at their destination.

There were many of these buses bringing people to the meeting, tens of thousands of people arriving to see this man on this night alone. Despite the heat, Lewis's father was wearing his suit. He'd put a clean hankie in the jacket's top pocket; the tip poked out like a tongue or a flag of surrender. He'd polished his shoes, combed his hair and had a shave. He was wearing Brylcreem and cologne. He looked like a man going on a date. All he needed was a bunch of flowers clutched in his hand. He had smartened Lewis up too, fussing over him as if grooming him to be presented to someone important. He'd insisted on clean underwear, just as his mother always did except that was more for getting run over in, for the doctors to see. (She was equally mindful of firemen. Lewis would have chosen to sleep naked but his mother said he had to wear pyjamas because if the house burnt down in the night he did not want to have to go outside with nothing on, for the firemen to see him like that, in all his glory, did he?)

Inside the stadium, this crowd, the like of which Lewis had never seen before, waited. They reminded him of himself perched on the branch of a tree, wanting to jump off and just fly. If only you could want it hard enough it might really happen. His father marvelled at the vast choir and hoped that he might hear his favourite hymn sung by so many voices, 'He Is Mine' filling up the space.

When Billy Graham came forward to the microphones to lead a prayer, there was a hush, and then he spoke, and he sounded to Lewis like a politician announcing that the world was at war. He talked, though, about the forgiveness of sin, while Lewis's father, sitting up very straight, sitting very still, listened intently. Lewis dared not make a sound. Silently, he sucked his sweets to nothing.

When the moment came—when he was called, while the choir was singing—his father got to his feet and went to the front in his wedding suit. Lewis almost followed him but by the time he'd thought about it, he'd lost sight of his father and Lewis was still in his seat.

While Lawrence was up, he made friends with a local couple. He introduced them to Lewis after the service. 'This is Lilian,' he said, of a young woman in a gay dress, and Lewis said, 'Pleased to meet you, ma'am,' as if, said Lawrence, shaking his head, he thought he were Elvis Presley. Lewis had put out a hand but Lilian laughed at it, reaching out to pinch his cheek instead. 'And this is John.' Lewis, turning to Lilian's husband, did not say, 'Pleased to meet you, sir,' or hold out his hand. He did not say or do anything, he just looked at John, who was looking back at him with bright blue eyes, and Lewis can hardly believe to this day that blue in an iris is an *absence* of colour. It was so hard not to stare at this startling blue; it was so hard to look away.

Lilian, meanwhile, was saying to Lawrence, continuing a conversation they had started before, 'You must come. We want you to. Do join us.'

'It's very kind of you,' said Lawrence, 'but my son and I have a bus to catch.' He put his hand on Lewis's shoulder and Lewis prepared to leave, but still these three stood talking and when Lewis and his father went to look for their bus, it appeared to have gone.

'We don't live very far away,' said Lilian, who had walked along with them. 'Come and spend the night with us.'

'That's very kind of you,' said Lawrence again, and Lewis waited for his father to say, 'but that won't be necessary,' but instead he said, 'thank you.'

The couple led the way to their car. 'You're welcome to stay for as long as you need,' said Lilian.

'We're a bit out of town,' said John, 'but I'll drive you to the train station when you're ready to go.'

Lewis and his father were driven through what remained of that June day to a house on the outskirts of the city. As he drove, John talked about the help he could do with in the garden, digging up the vegetables, and about the animals they had, so that Lewis was picturing a big house surrounded by land, a long, dusty driveway with chickens running around, a veranda at the front and a number of dogs. He was surprised to arrive at a small house with a square of tarmac at the front and a cramped garden behind, not a dog or a chicken to be seen.

They were shown inside, directly into a sitting room. Invited to make themselves comfortable, they sat down on the large sofa, whose brightly coloured fabric was covered in protective plastic that creaked beneath them. A magnificent chandelier hung from the high ceiling, dominating the small room. Beneath it, on a table, was a goldfish in a bowl.

Lilian went to the kitchen and came back carrying a tray. In order to put it down, she pushed the fish to one end of the table, the water sloshing violently inside the little bowl. She handed out glasses of flat lemonade before sitting down in a plastic-covered armchair. She shut her eyes and for a moment Lewis thought that she had gone to sleep, but then she fanned her face with her short fingers, made an exclamation about the heat, and called for the dog. They talked about the meeting in the stadium. Lewis's father said, 'I'm a new man.'

'I'm full of light,' said Lilian.

John turned his blue eyes on Lewis. 'And how about you, Lewis?' he said.

Lewis, swallowing his flat lemonade, shrugged and said that nothing had really happened to him in there.

'Don't you want to give your heart to Jesus?' said John. 'Don't you want to know that you're going to heaven?'

'It will come,' said Lilian. 'Give it time.' She called again for the dog. 'It's as hot as hell in here,' she said. Catching her husband's chiding glance, she added, 'It really is hot.'

The side window was open and a whirring fan stood near it, facing out, as if to keep the sultry air from getting inside in the first place.

Lilian poured more lemonade and said, 'This room gets all the sunshine and gets so hot the dog won't come in here.' She called again, more insistently, but there was no sign or sound of the dog.

John said to Lawrence, 'So tell me where you come from,' and Lawrence told him about the house on Small Street, but he was talking about his childhood, his Uncle Ted, a widower, 'who,' he said, 'I loved more than I loved my own father,' and his handsome cousin Bertie who was like the brother Lawrence did not have.

Lawrence asked about baptism. 'Can it even be done at my age?' he asked.

'It's never too late,' said John.

Lewis was picturing a font, a dribble of water on the forehead, but, said John, it would not be like that. Lawrence would be immersed. When he came out of the water, it would be as if he were entering the world anew.

When they had finished the lemonade, Lilian showed them the spare bedrooms. Of the smaller one, the box room, in which Lewis was to sleep, Lilian said, 'The window sometimes slides open a crack. If it bothers you, just tell John and he'll come and nail it shut for you. The dog will sometimes sleep in here so just keep your door closed if you don't want him to.'

Lewis left the door open. When he woke, wearing no pyjamas, in the middle of the night, he did not know where he was. He thought that he had fallen asleep closer to home. He was remembering the sound of horses' hooves on the road outside, ringing through the still afternoon, echoing off the houses, sounding like the drum beat of a samba band, as if there were a carnival; he thought that he had heard an ice cream van playing 'Greensleeves' in his sleep. When he realised where he was he felt lonely.

Lying in John and Lilian's spare bed somewhere near Manchester, Lewis listened for the sounds of the city just outside, but he couldn't even hear the dog. He wanted the night air to come in, bringing the city with it, but the night air was unmoving and even at dawn the only sounds that came in were birdsong and the milkman doing his rounds. Lewis, who wanted to feel that he was on the brink of the city, and who had wanted the dog to come in and sleep on his bed, was disappointed.

In the morning, he expected to leave, but instead, after breakfast, his father offered to help John in the back garden. What they harvested was cooked by Lilian for the evening meal, and then it was bedtime again. When Lewis woke from those dreams of his, he found on the floor a pair of underpants and a T-shirt that did not belong to him.

'Did you find them?' asked Lilian, when he got downstairs. 'I put some of John's things on the end of your bed. You can wear them while yours are in the laundry.' And so they stayed another day and another night, and again Lewis slept with both the window and the door slightly open, but he did not see the dog. It seemed to feed at night when the house was cooler. Lilian went from the sweltering kitchen where she laboured to the stifling front room to rest. John spent all day in the small garden, stripped to the waist in the sunshine. He should have been a pioneer farmer, thought Lewis, seeing him resting with one foot on the edge of his spade. He could imagine John standing in the middle of a cornfield in Canada or Australia in the 1800s, holding a scythe or the reins of a horse.

In his garden, John dug up small potatoes and skinny carrots. He picked fruit from the dwarf apple tree and the gooseberry bush, and Lilian turned the fruit into pies with not quite enough sugar in. Lawrence helped him, and Lewis would have helped too but he found it too hot and avoided doing anything much during the day. Instead, he sat on the shady front steps, gazing in the direction of the city or watching the birds flying overhead, watching them land. He thought about migration, about birds that were programmed to fly south to France, and he wondered if they ever wanted to fly further than they should, whether any bird had ever tried to cross the Atlantic and found that it could not get that far in one go.

He hung around in the kitchen, doing small jobs for Lilian, slowly, standing at the sink.

'How old are you?' asked Lilian.

'I'm eighteen,' said Lewis.

'He's already drinking,' said Lawrence, coming into the kitchen with John, and the three of them stood there looking at Lewis until he had to turn away and still he felt the burn of their gaze on the back of his neck; he thought he could hear their heads shaking.

Lilian made her own lemonade and jam, and John pickled his own beetroot. Lewis had rather expected to discover that they made their own home brew, but none ever appeared. In fact, Lewis discovered that John was a man who poured gifts of alcohol down the sink, leaving the kitchen rich with the scent of the wasted wine. Lewis had never had wine. He had not yet found anything he liked to drink, unless he mixed lemonade in with lager. He would have liked a cold shandy while he sat out on the steps, like the man of the house, like a rancher, watching the sun set. Instead, Lilian brought out tumblers of juice, saying to him, 'Take these to the men, would you?' Lewis took two tumblers around the side of the house, towards the back garden where the men were working. As he approached the corner, he heard their voices, his father and John talking. 'He's got this friend,' his father was saying. 'He's a bad influence. He's got Lewis drinking and I don't know what else they get up to.'

'Are they going with girls?' said John.

'No,' said his father. 'Not girls.'

There was a pause in which nothing was said, and then John said, 'Ah.'

Later, Lewis ran a deep bath and lay in the water with his shoulders and knees sticking out. He thought about baptism and how one could access a bright new world. Could it happen when you were naked, he wondered, or only when you had your clothes on, a clean pair of pants? Could it happen when you were alone or did someone else have to be there, immersing you? There probably had to be a reading from the Bible; what came to mind were the Thou Shalt Nots, the rules of behaviour: *Thou shalt not kill, Thou shalt not commit adultery, Thou shalt not steal, Thou shalt not bear false witness, Thou shalt not covet (anything?* he wondered), and, *Thou shalt not lie with mankind, as with womankind: it is abomination.*

In the morning, they said their goodbyes to Lilian at the door before going with John into Manchester. Lilian called for the dog to come and see them off too, but when they left she was still calling.

Lewis sat in the back of the car, wearing his own underpants and his own shirt. It was early and there was not much sign of life in the streets through which John drove them. He brought them into the city centre just as it began to get lively, delivering them to the bustling station just in time for them to leave.

HE WANTS TO FEEL
AN EARTHQUAKE

LEWIS HANGS HIS dressing gown on the back of his bedroom door. He puts on clean underwear (*You never know*, his mother would say, *who's going to see it.*) and a clean shirt. Buckling the belt of his trousers, he sits down on the end of the double bed and appraises himself in the dressing-table mirror. He wears sideburns and keeps his hair long. Edie sometimes tried to persuade him to have a trim, to shave off his sideburns. 'You'd look so much younger,' she said. 'You look like a mountain man.' (Lewis liked this idea, and tried to see it in his reflection—a mountain man, but with glasses, and soft hands.) He calls his eye colour 'hazel' because he thought he saw a little green in the irises once, perhaps when he had a suntan, but he can't see it now. He hasn't had a decent tan for years. Perhaps he ought to just call his eyes 'brown', as others do. His glasses have thick rims that make him look as if he is wearing a disguise, as if his large nose might be attached to the bridge of the glasses, as if it might be just as removable. Ruth discovered contact lenses and said that he should try them too. Lewis, though, picturing his short-haired, clean-faced, clear-eyed self, thought that he would look like a grown man trying to pass himself off as a schoolboy, like Frédéric Bourdin.

He combs his hair and goes to check his emails. He has his computer in Ruth's old room, on the desk she used to use for her schoolwork. There is an uncomfortable wooden chair on which he sits. He turns the computer on and waits.

All over Ruth's bedroom walls, there are posters of young men who were famous when Lewis was a boy. One of them is wearing a lumberjack shirt and has his thumbs hooked into the belt of his denim trousers. He is smiling, showing his neat, white teeth. Lewis's sister used to have posters of Cliff Richard on her bedroom walls. Every night, she went to sleep listening to his records. Lewis once went with her to a concert and saw grown women fainting when Cliff Richard came on stage in his shiny suit. She would have married Cliff Richard if she could. On her wedding day, she walked down the aisle to 'Bachelor Boy'.

Lewis has been looking through old albums recently, unearthing photos that he has not looked at in decades—himself and Edie with Ruth as a baby, and before Ruth, in bright honeymoon Polaroids, and prior to that a decade of snaps of Edie in her early thirties, her late twenties, her early twenties when they first met in the library. And in the last album he looked in, he discovered himself as a single young man, and as a boy at school. He studied a photo of his sixth form class, finding his adolescent self standing at the right-hand end of the front row with his eyes closed. Mostly, he struggled to put names to faces, but when he scanned the back row and saw the boy who stood at the left-hand end, he knew that boy's name instantly. For years, probably decades, Lewis believed that Sydney was the capital of Australia.

Sydney Flynn had not arrived at Lewis's school until the sixth form. Born abroad, Sydney had moved around a lot with his family, his father being an army man, an older father who had then taken early retirement. Lewis had been struck by Sydney's height, his bone structure, his blond hair, which came together to give him the look, thought Lewis, of Flash Gordon.

Lewis wanted to have been born abroad, or at least in a city, anywhere but Small Street.

Sydney sat at the back of the class, behind Lewis. Sydney called him Lewie, or Louise. Lewis sometimes felt the nib of Sydney's pen poking into the back of his neck. He did not know whether Sydney was trying to be friendly or to hurt him. Turning around, he did not know whether to smile or glare.

At home, Lewis would stand in front of the bathroom mirror holding his mother's hand mirror behind his head, and he would look at these dots of dark ink on the back of his neck, studying them as if they were some kind of message.

Sometimes, in class, when Lewis felt that pen nib touching the back of his neck, and he turned, he found Sydney looking not at him but at his own sums, his head bent low over his work, and when he got home and looked for ink marks on the back of his neck, he would see that nothing was there.

Sydney had a younger brother whom he adored and terrorised. Sydney boasted about waking his brother in horrible ways, setting alarm clocks to go off in the early hours and hiding them around his brother's bedroom and under the floorboards. His brother came to school with a moustache inked onto his upper lip, or with one eyebrow missing. Lewis imagined what it would be like to be Sydney's brother, always knowing that when you opened your eyes in the morning, Sydney might be there by your bed, with a pen or a razor in his hand, and you would know that something had happened, or was about to happen.

Sydney once bit a boy's ear in the playground, in a brutal play fight that Lewis watched, along with at least fifty others who cheered the boys on. Afterwards, Sydney shook the boy's hand. On another occasion, Lewis saw Sydney take a tin soldier from a younger boy, put it in his own pocket and take it home. The boy made only the slightest protest and looked, thought Lewis, quite proud. Alone at home, Lewis thought about this sinking of teeth into flesh. He thought about this stealing of other boys' valuables, kept warm inside Sydney's pockets. Lewis had valuables too but Sydney never stole anything from him; Lewis always had to take them home again.

Sometimes, Sydney cycled past him, singing out, 'Louie Louie'. Lewis, at that time, had not heard the song. A few years later, he heard the Kingsmen's version, and at the same time heard the rumour that the song was obscenely sexual, although apparently the only way to make out the words was by playing the single at 33⅓ RPM. He did this, but he still could not fathom what was sung. It was so dirty, it was said, that the lyrics were investigated by the FBI. It turned out that there was nothing improper secreted in the song, whose lyrics were not filthy but sweet, all about a sailor sailing home to the girl he loved. When Lewis discovered this, he was disappointed.

Edie, who only came to the village in her twenties, never met Sydney, who was long gone by then. When Lewis and Edie finally came to arrange their wedding, Lewis, thinking about his best man, thought of Sydney, his poking pen and the brother whom he terrorised. He imagined that Sydney would be the kind of best man to put Lewis on a long-distance train or handcuff him naked to a lamp post or shave off his eyebrows the night before the wedding, who would have him turning up at the church without his trousers, with his buttocks tattooed. He asked Edie's brother, a reliable man, to fill the role. On his stag night, Lewis kept waiting for the handcuffs to appear, for something unexpected to occur, but nothing did, nothing happened at all. When the wedding was over, Edie's brother tied to the bumper of Lewis's car a pair of old slippers that dragged behind them for miles, all the way from the church hall to the Peak District without making a sound.

When the computer is ready, Lewis opens up his email, finding new messages in bold. Someone he knows—a friend of his or someone he's acquainted with—keeps sending him pictures, but Ruth says he mustn't open them, he mustn't look. 'That's not a friend,' she says. One email says he's due thousands of pounds, but there is a link he must click on to claim the money, and he daren't. 'Incompetent in love,' says another. He does not want cheap Viagra or SuperViagra; he does not want bigger, harder, longer-lasting erections. He does not want a nineteen-year-old Russian girl or an Australian virgin who wants to talk. He does not want a replica Rolex watch or a fake Gucci handbag. He does not want a pair of modestly priced cufflinks ('a dream come true'). He does not want these dazzling boons. He does not want the Federal Government of Nigeria to transfer fifteen million United States Dollars into his bank account; he does not want three million, five hundred thousand

Great British Pounds from the Manager of Gulf International Bank. He moves these emails to the rubbish bin.

He has complained to Ruth about the spam. 'I don't want all this,' he said to her. 'How do I stop it?'

'I don't know,' she said. 'I'm not sure you can.'

While she watched, he clicked on 'Get Mail', downloading a message that said, 'Feeble in bed'.

He goes onto the Internet. It was in his retirement, and after he stopped driving, that he got a computer and learnt to use the World Wide Web, to google. He checks the news and the weather. He tries to keep up. He becomes anxious if he does not see the news for a while; he wonders what he is missing. He once stayed with Edie on a farm in the Lake District. They had a cottage with no radio, no television, no phone. They saw the farmer's wife on arrival and then did not see her again. They saw the farmer going by in his tractor, the tires six feet tall. They saw the odd stranger as they hiked beneath the mountains. Crossing a small stone bridge (with moss growing on its walls and fleece clinging to the moss—straggly white strands, slightly kinked like pubic hairs) they passed a man who smiled at them, opened his arms to the warm day, and said as he passed them, 'Very fucking pleasant.'

It was indeed pleasant. Their cottage, though, was in the middle of nowhere and they had none of the things they needed for self-catering—no dish soap, no tea towel, no dustpan and broom. (It was only on the day they left that they found a cupboard containing all the things they had needed during the week.) There was no newsagent selling newspapers. Arriving home, they discovered that there had been riots up and down the country, starting in London and spreading like a forest fire to the Midlands and then to the north. On hearing the news, Lewis felt a flush of excitement, and at the same time a touch of disappointment at not having realised it was happening until it was already over.

When Lewis woke up one morning not long after that and realised that Edie had died in her sleep, he felt as if he had come home to find his front door kicked open, his windows smashed, everything gone. He felt as if he had slept through an earthquake.

He does sleep through earthquakes. There was one very recently, with a magnitude of three, right where he lives but he was unaware of it until he read about it in the paper in due course. He would like to experience an earthquake, to feel the ground shaking beneath him, to feel the bed trembling, all the ornaments rattling like something out of an exorcism.

He opens up Google and, with one finger, types in 'Sydney Flynn'. He clicks 'search', and Google returns more than seven million results. He looks through the first few pages but they are not the Sydney Flynn he is after. 'Sydney Flynn' is on Facebook, Twitter, MySpace, Pinterest, YouTube and Google+, but they all seem to be women. He tries some variations on his search criteria, finding an obituary that makes his heart seem to stop, but it is not his Sydney Flynn and he feels his heart start beating again. The only other link that looks promising takes him to a site that says 'Page Not Found' and no matter how many times he clicks on the link, he cannot access the page he wants.

He has not spoken to Sydney since the summer of 1961. On New Year's Eve in the year of the riots, the year Edie died, the school hosted a reunion for pupils who had left fifty years before. Lewis went along, although not in the fancy dress that some people wore for the occasion—wigs, also chest wigs beneath wide-collared shirts, flared trousers and platform shoes. They'd worn nothing like this at the time, or ever in their lives, so why do it now, wondered Lewis, when they were old men, when it just made them look foolish? Lewis wore his normal clothes. He wore a clean shirt (whose collar was nearly as wide as some of the men's joke shirts). He combed his hair (which was almost as long as some of the men's centre-parted 'hippie' wigs). He thought he might see Sydney there. The few familiar faces, though, were those he already knew from the pub, the old boys with whom he drank in The Golden Fleece—because back then he could still go there. They were the ones who had stayed in the village, and some of their children had stayed, and some of them had grandchildren at the school. Lewis wandered into the school hall. The houselights were down. Up on the stage, a DJ was just getting started. A disco ball had been hung from the ceiling and as it spun, spots of light crossed the empty dance floor and it was like a sky full of shooting stars. (This was the dinner hall really, transformed for the evening. Lewis could almost smell—through the illusion of the music and lights—the food and the mop bucket. He imagined stray chips and peas on the floor, being trodden on by dancing couples and adhering to the soles of their shoes.) He kept thinking, as he walked around the room, that he heard people saying Sydney's name, but he did not see him anywhere. Towards the end of the evening, when Sydney had not shown up and the DJ had come to the end of the 1960s tunes and was playing 'The Final Countdown', Lewis left the school hall. He walked away from the couples who were slow-dancing beneath the spinning disco ball, and headed down the corridor towards the classrooms, in which his father had taught English Literature until he could no longer bear to, and in which Lewis had taught Religious Studies for more than forty years, and into which Sydney had arrived more than half a century before. It was almost midnight. There would be a pantomime flash and a BOOM! and a cloud of smoke and glitter and, like a golden coach that was really a pumpkin, the dance hall—with the houselights turned on and the disco ball turned off (*Pack up the stars*, thought Lewis, *dismantle the sun*)—would become, once more, the place where school dinners were eaten.

After shutting down the computer, Lewis sits for a while looking around Ruth's room. Her shelves are empty of the classics that belong there, the stories he read as a boy, stories in which you can walk through a mirror or through the back of a wardrobe or climb to the top of a tree and find an unlikely and magical land. He used to try it, half closing his eyes and stepping forward, walking so hopefully, with such desire, into his mirror, into the back of his wardrobe. He could never get in. He read these stories to Ruth when she was little, and he supposes she has taken them to read to her boy. In the children's television programmes she used to watch, a man passed through a changing room door into another world; and a boy, put to bed by his mother, used his torch to open up a portal in his bedroom floor, sliding with his dog down a helter-skelter into Cuckoo Land.

She has left the posters. Where Ruth lives now, she has magnolia walls hung with monochrome studio portraits of her family. These men in their unbuttoned lumberjack shirts, these men with whom she was briefly in love when she was young, grin down at Lewis now.

A dreamcatcher dangles from the ceiling.

He looks at his watch, and at the same time removes it from his wrist. It aggravates the skin where his arm got burned and increasingly he finds himself leaving it off.

It is almost opening time. Not much more than a year ago, he might have been going to The Golden

Fleece now, but not any longer. These days he goes to another pub in the opposite direction. It is not as popular with the locals but Miranda is friendly. He thinks that he would like to be able to say to Ruth, when she comes round in the morning, that he did go out of the house, and not just to the bin.

Leaving his watch next to the computer, he gets up out of the uncomfortable chair and heads downstairs.

HE DOES NOT WANT
THE SAUSAGES

At the bottom of the stairs, Lewis stops to take his coat down from the peg. The buttons are coming off—they are hanging by threads, and one is missing altogether. His gloves are in the pockets. Holding on to the banister, he lowers himself onto the second stair, where he takes off his slippers and puts on his outdoor shoes. Standing again, he pauses to check that he has his key and to put on his hat, and then he heads outside, stopping to slam the door behind him. He sometimes has to slam it three times before it closes properly. If he does not, he might come home and find his door standing wide open.

He goes carefully down the front steps and onto the path of concrete slabs. He laid the slabs himself when he and Edie first came to this house, along with the garden walls at the front and back. Eyeing the grass on either side, passing the stone lion at the gate, he looks up the road. A hundred yards away are the public toilets. A sign on the wall of the toilet block says, 'THESE FACILITIES ARE FOR ALL TO USE', and, beneath a picture of a family of four rounded stick people, 'IS YOUR CONDUCT APPROPRIATE?' Beyond the toilets is The Golden Fleece. He turns in the opposite direction and wanders down the road towards the other pub. He goes slowly, scanning the pavement for his missing button.

Everything is quiet. There is a spit of rain in the air. It reminds him of the seaside, the salt spray when the tide comes in and the sea pounds against the wall as if it cannot accept that this is as far as it goes.

His grandparents lived on the coast. They had a beach hut until it was lost in a storm. Lewis had imagined a whirlwind lifting it neatly out of the row, whisking it intact into the sky, like the little wooden house in *The Wizard of Oz*.

He always imagined living by the sea, perhaps in his retirement. But he is now seventy years old, retired years ago, and is still living in this village in the Midlands, less than a mile from the house in which he grew up and around the corner from the school in which he has spent the best part of his life.

His parents' house on Small Street is gone now, knocked down to build the supermarket parking lot, which has signs around the perimeter that say, 'Motorists! Your car is at risk from thieves' and, 'Leave it on show expect it to go'. The pub is half a mile ahead, but Lewis turns right, towards the school. When he reaches the school railings, he stops, gazing into the deserted playground. When the double doors open, he flinches in anticipation of the headmistress striding out, coming towards him. His instinct is to run, as if he were not a grown-up, a previous employee of this establishment, but a truant, a runaway, an absentee who might be dragged by the ear to the headmistress's office. It is not the headmistress, though; it is a boy, going from one building to another, perhaps with a message for a teacher or a wound for the school nurse. Lewis thinks for a moment that it is a boy he knows, but then he realises that it is not, that it can't be, because all the children he knew will have gone by now.

Lewis turns away, walking on in the direction of the pub. Passing a bus shelter, he thinks about Ruth and her saying to him, 'You can travel for free all over the country—what are you waiting for?' He could go to the seaside; he could go all the way to Dover. He will do it, he thinks, one of these days. Not right now. He would want to wait for warmer weather. He would need to apply for a bus pass. He would have to go into town to get a passport photo taken.

You are not allowed to smile in your photo any more.

He stops to watch a yellow car go by, turning to meet the gaze of the dog that is staring at him through the rear window, its mouth open and fixed in a smile. The car, a Saab, stops at the pedestrian crossing a little further along the road, letting across a woman with hair that is grey at the roots and dyed red at the ends. Lewis starts walking back towards it, but the yellow car is already moving again. Turning the corner, it goes out of sight.

Lewis is still gazing at that empty corner when he realises that the woman for whom the car stopped, the woman who crossed the road, is now very near. She comes, in her dogtooth coat, to a stop just in front of him. Lewis is lifting the hat off his head when the woman raises her hand and strikes him sufficiently hard that his glasses fly off his face. He is still holding his hat in the air; his mouth is still slightly open, ready to speak. He saw, before he lost his glasses, the scarring on her face, the damage to her skin. She starts shouting, jabbing at his chest with her index finger, and he realises who she is, and he, apologising, replaces his hat and reaches down to the ground for his glasses. While the woman is standing there telling him off, Lewis returns his glasses to his face but finds that the lenses are smashed and takes them off again. He puts them in his pocket and walks away as quickly as his poorly knee will allow.

Just outside the pub, he sees what he thinks for a moment might be his button lying on the ground, but then he remembers that it is a pound coin; it has been there for months. The first time he saw it, he stopped to reach down and pick it up and found that it was glued to the pavement. He remembers his confusion, his scrabbling fingertips. He remembers when Ruth's boy was a baby and would try to get hold of things that could not be grasped, that could not be picked up—a biscuit pictured on the lid of a tin, a dot of light on the living-room carpet. Lewis, scratching at the pavement, had to straighten up again and walk on without it.

The pub always looks closed from the outside, but when he pushes open the heavy door there is light and sound and Miranda smiling at him as the door settles behind him. The interior reminds him of somebody's living room. The wallpaper shows quaint farming scenes, a man with a scythe surveying his land, the pattern repeating around the four walls. There is a busy carpet, a threadbare sofa, sport on a small television in the corner and a handful of classic board games on a table underneath. There are floral curtains, vases of plastic daffodils on the windowsills, ornaments on the mantelpiece above the fireplace in which logs are arranged as if ready to be lit, although they never are. There are shelves containing ancient hardback books that no one reads: *Todhunter's Differential Calculus*, three volumes of Harmsworth's *Home Doctor: BRU–DUC, DUL–JEA* and *POW–SYS*, and Carter's *Outlines of History* in which history stops in 1918. Lewis wonders if there are later editions in which history instead comes to an end in 1945 or 1961 or 2013. There are two copies of *Les Misérables* and faded children's classics, a beautiful old edition of a little book of nursery rhymes that he had when he was a boy. *Topsy-turvy, upside down, the sea is on the moon.* He doesn't know where his copy has gone. Sydney would just take this one.

There is no clock. Sometimes the pub has lock-ins. With the door bolted and the curtains closed, you can lose your sense of time. Each time he enters, he half expects to smell Woodbines, to see, through a smoky haze, an old man sucking on a cigarette, the ash dropping off, the end of the cigarette smouldering. There is no smoking in the pubs, though, these days.

When Lewis has made his way across the room, Miranda says to him, 'What do you want, love?'

Yes, he wants to say to her, *yes, please.*

Taking his hat off and putting it down on the bar, he asks for a shandy. While she is pulling his half, she says to him, 'I didn't win.' She means the lottery. Lewis has seen the advert, the giant hand in the sky, a formation of stars, the finger pointing, 'It could be you'. He hasn't seen it for a while though. He has a feeling all of that's long gone now; there'll be a new slogan. Miranda plays every Saturday but has won nothing yet. 'The minute I do,' she says, 'I'm out of here.' Edie used to play at work, in a pool. At least once, maybe twice, they won ten pounds and shared it between them.

Lewis asks about the sausages.

'We've only got vegetarian,' she says.

He makes a face.

'Pork and blood pudding next week.'

'I've never had blood pudding.'

Miranda puts his drink down on the bar and turns to another customer who has come in, who is asking for Goldschläger. 'We don't have that,' says Miranda. They watch the man turn away and then Miranda says to Lewis, 'Have you ever had Goldschläger?'

'No,' he says.

'It's a Swiss liqueur,' she says, 'with bits of gold in it, flakes of gold leaf.' As she says this, she is touching the flimsy gold necklace that she wears around her neck, tapping the tiny crucifix against her throat.

'Have you ever had it?' asks Lewis, taking a sip of his shandy.

'No,' she says.

Lewis shakes his head. What kind of a man, he thinks, walks around asking for Swiss liqueurs with bits of gold in? He stands at the bar with his drink, thinking about the things he's never had and never will.

'What are you going to have, then?' asks Miranda.

'I don't want the vegetarian ones,' he says. He reaches for a menu and Miranda moves down the bar to serve someone else. Without his glasses, though, he cannot read it. When Miranda comes back, Lewis says to her, 'I haven't got my glasses. What else have you got?'

'Home-made steak and kidney pudding,' she says, and Lewis brightens up. 'But I just sold the last one.'

Lewis turns to look at the man who is moving away from the bar, who is scanning the room for a table he wants, and Lewis sees, with a rush of indignation, that it is him, the Goldschläger man, who has decided to eat instead and is settling down now at a corner table, waiting for his suet pudding to arrive.

The pub uses a local butcher. They know exactly, they say, what is in their meat products. Lewis remembers when Ruth went on a school trip to France and was given sausages that were—she discovered after eating them—made of horsemeat. She was furious, and Edie was furious, and Lewis pretended to be furious too. But when, more recently, the news broke that horsemeat had been found in frozen meat products, Lewis went to the supermarket, wondering about buying some. He was disappointed to find that they had already been removed from the freezers.

Lewis, for his lunch, has a pickled egg. When Miranda is not busy, she comes and stands near him. 'Let me cut your hair,' she says.

'I haven't had my hair short since I was in my teens,' says Lewis.

'I'll take years off you.'

'It was halfway down my back when I got married.'

'Let me take the ends off,' she says, walking away and returning with a pair of heavy scissors, snipping at the air as she approaches.

It was touching his shoulders when he met Edie.

'Cut it to my shoulders,' he says.

She pulls out a chair, sits him down, and gives him a haircut right there in the bar. Long hanks of grey fall onto the carpet, and he has the sense that she is chopping the grey off, that when she has finished what will be left will be brown.

'Cut it short,' he says.

She is cutting it to the nape of his neck when she says, 'Have you had this mole looked at?' Standing aside, she touches it with the tip of her long scissors, like a weather girl pointing out a weather front, and Lewis remembers his three o'clock appointment and what it is for.

'I'm having it cut out,' he says, 'this afternoon.'

'That's good,' she says.

He notices that she completes his haircut without touching the back of his neck.

When she has finished, when his hair is lying in a circle around him like a nest, he peers into the pickled-egg jar, trying to see his reflection, but it is unclear. Staring into the depths of the jar, he says to Miranda, 'Byron consumed vinegar on a daily basis. He believed in its health benefits. He ate potatoes soaked in vinegar.'

Miranda looks at the slightly cloudy, pale-yellow liquid inside the jar that holds the eggs. 'I know someone who drinks his own wee for the same reason,' she says.

Lewis does not have his watch on but he feels that time is pressing. Leaving the last half inch of his shandy, he prepares to leave. 'Thanks for the cut,' he says to Miranda, reaching up to touch the surprising softness of his crop, the neat bristle around his ears. In the doorway, as he exits, he passes a young man who is on his way in. For a moment, they are holding the same bit of the door; the young man's hand is on top of Lewis's. The way he is dressed reminds Lewis of the Teddy Boys of his youth. He never saw a real one but he has seen pictures. Once, when Ruth was in her teens and interested in youth culture, Lewis told her that he had been in Manchester in the sixties, and she was impressed. When she questioned him about it, he was oblique.

He went back, once, to see Lilian and John, taking Edie and Ruth along. He drove up to Manchester, to the outskirts, trying to remember the route, to recognise where he was. 'What are you looking for?' asked Edie, and Lewis could hardly tell her. When, finally, he stood on the steps on which he had spent so many hours just sitting, and when he knocked on the front door, he did not know what he would say. He was expecting Lilian to come to the door, but it was John who answered. Eighteen years old when he had first met John, Lewis was then in his early fifties and realised with surprise that John was not much older than him; he was no more than sixty. He had seemed so much older when Lewis was young. Ruth, at seventeen, did not want to be there—'I've got things to do, places to be,' she said, although there did not seem to be anything specific—but John turned his bright blue eyes on her and said, 'Please come in,' and they all went inside.

Without making eye contact, the young man who is dressed like a Teddy Boy moves his hand and squeezes by, disappearing into the pub.

Outside, the pavement is dry. The spit of rain has come to nothing. Lewis touches his pocket, feeling the shape and weight of the little book of nursery rhymes stowed inside. *Arsey-versey, back to front, the past will be here soon.*

As he nears his house, he hears the sound of a plane going overhead. Looking up, concentrating on the sky, he does not see the yellow Saab parked by the curb just in front of his house.

HE WANTS A
CUP OF TEA

THE WALLS OF the nursing home used to be painted
pink, 'Drunk-tank pink,' said Lewis on one of his first
visits. 'That's the colour they painted the cells where
prisoners are put to cool off.' You would think, he
added, looking around, that everyone in this place had
done something wrong and was being given some
time to think about it.

The shade was believed to induce calm. When the
manager learnt that the shade was instead suspected of, over time, increasing agitation, the pink was
painted over with lavender. The manager hopes that
the new colour in the corridors—these lavender tun-
nels—will prove to be soothing to the residents.

There are pictures hanging on the walls—small
watercolours of boats in harbours, of woodland in
the autumn, of setting suns. There is no modern art,

nothing that, like a Rorschach image, might be open to interpretation.

The furniture is rounded or cushioned; there are no sharp corners. Some of the wood is real and when it is polished the whole place smells of Mr Sheen. There is a CD player on an oval table in the corner of the communal living room. The CDs one can choose from are of birdsong and dolphin song and the sound of the sea.

Lawrence, who has had his midday soup and white-bread sandwiches, who is full of preservatives, is sitting in one of the two dozen beige, wipe-clean chairs. He is waiting for someone to come. He is not sure who, or perhaps what—maybe this is the day the dog comes. He knows, though, that someone or something is coming.

It is not Sunday, when Lewis comes and takes him to the nearby church. Lawrence was baptised long ago but Lewis is still deciding whether or not he is ready. He is afraid, thinks Lawrence, of what will happen. He is not afraid of the baptism itself, of being submerged, although he never was confident in the water. It is the promise of entering into a bright new world that makes him anxious. Lawrence imagines his son worrying about finding himself there without something he needs—his gloves, perhaps. Lewis is afraid of the Eucharist, the taking of the body and the drinking of the blood of Christ. It is not just that he does not like the wine. 'I'm sure,' Lawrence has said, 'you could have juice instead.' But Lewis seems to be afraid of giving himself completely, of surrendering his heart. Since childhood, he has been afraid of the idea that God can see deep down inside him. He sometimes avoided Sunday school, feigning illness, claiming to have stomach cramps that Lawrence did not believe in for a moment.

Lawrence has a good singing voice. At home, in the house on Small Street, he liked to sing in the bath, belting out hymns through the steam. Here, the baths they run for the residents are not so deep, and they don't let the water get hot enough to steam up the room, and besides, they leave the bathroom door wide open. He only sings in church now. Lawrence would very much like to hear the organist striking up the first few notes of 'He Is Mine' but it has never happened. He has made a note to have it sung at his funeral. He would like to see a performance of Handel's *Messiah*. He has asked Lewis to buy him the CD but it has not yet appeared; Lewis seems to be having some problem getting hold of it.

Every Sunday, after church, on the way back to the nursing home, Lewis stops at the newsagent's, the sweet shop. He stands there looking at the jars on the shelves—huge plastic jars full of all sorts of brightly coloured sweets—choosing what he wants. When Lewis was small, Lawrence used to say to him, 'You're all want.' Lewis was always calling for his mother. 'I want you to come,' he would shout, when he was three, four years old, sitting on his bottom in the middle of the room, 'I want you to come here now.' But then, when she went to him, he would not be able to say what he wanted her for. Lawrence does not see why Lewis has to stand for so long looking, trying to decide, when in the end he always buys the same thing, the same sweets every week.

'Oh,' says Lawrence.

It is not his birthday, he is sure of that. On the wall just inside the kitchen, there is a list of names and dates, days on which there will be birthday cake. Through this one and that one a pencil line has been drawn, indicating the passing not of the birthday but of the birthday girl or boy. Lawrence, who has seen this list, wonders about the use of pencil, which seems rather tentative, non-committal. Hanging from a string, there is a pencil with a rubber on the end, in case of mistakes, he supposes; in case, he likes to say to the nurses, God does not want them and sends them back. His name is still on the list, a little way down, to-wards the end of the year; he has not yet been crossed out. He likes to go into the kitchen; he likes to see how clean they keep it. There are steel work surfaces. There is a vast fridge with shiny steel doors. Another appliance is full of steam that billows out when a steel door is pulled down. Lawrence is not allowed to go into the kitchen. When they find him in there, they take his arm. 'Inspection time, is it, Lawrence?' they say, looking at one another. 'Pass or fail?' And then they take him back to wherever he was.

He sees someone in the corridor—a lady, perhaps a nurse going by. Lawrence calls out but she does not hear him, or does not come anyway. 'I know you're there,' he says. He listens, hearing voices, hearing a fly that has got itself stuck to some flypaper. 'Where are you?'

Doris Bolton is sitting a few seats along from him, her small hands gripping the arms of her chair as if the nurses might want to take it away from her, just as they have taken, so she claims, her mother's silver hairbrush and her gramophone. Her son comes every day, just before teatime. He is very sweet to his mother, although Lawrence is aware of the boy's reputation and has noticed that some of the nurses are nervous around him. When Doris's boy leaves, he always takes the trouble to say goodbye to his mother's friends, as he calls them. He shakes Lawrence's hand; he knows him by name.

'Oh,' says Lawrence.

Doris is watching a home improvement programme on the television. The workers are in the garden, putting down black polythene to stop the grass and weeds growing through. They are spreading a ton of pebbles on top of the polythene, erecting bamboo fencing and installing a water feature, electrically driven running water. They are laying nonslip decking, putting up waterproof fairy lights and arranging outdoor furniture and pot plants so that the people will have somewhere nice to sit at the end of the day.

On these makeover programmes, they always go back a year later. Lawrence sometimes wonders if they wish they just hadn't looked, if they wish they had just done the job—laid the pebbles and the decking, cleaned the limescale off the sink and cleared out the fridge, thrown away the middle-aged lady's sequined tops and replaced them with the trouser suits that flatter her figure and her autumnal colouring—and then walked away, knowing that their work was done, that they had done some good. But they go back. They wait a year and then return, with the camera already filming as they stand on the front doorstep and knock. They can't help it, they have to look. They have to see the state of the garden now, the state of the kitchen; they have to see what the lady is wearing. They will find that the weeds are growing through despite the polythene. They will see the cat excrement in amongst the pebbles, the sticks of bamboo that have split and snapped, the half-dead plants flattened by footballs, the decking turning green. They will see the limescale on the sink, the double cream in the fridge. They will discover that the lady has been into the garbage bags, digging out a sequined top and wearing it to the karaoke on Thursday nights; they will find the autumnal trouser suits still hanging in the wardrobe, barely worn. They will be disappointed.

The house on Small Street had a back garden. No wider than the narrow house and only ten feet deep, it backed up against a field whose edges you could not even see and you could almost think of that as an extension of the garden, except that there was a wall between the two, and the field was private with no public right of way. Signs on the gate said, 'KEEP OUT' and, 'DOGS WILL BE SHOT'. You could see the field though, from the upstairs windows. A sizeable tree grew in the nearest corner. Its branches hung over the wall, dappling the bed in which Lewis planted apple pips that never grew into trees, and in which he tried to grow sunflowers faster than the slugs could eat them. The garden did not get much sunshine, but they put the stripy deckchairs out there anyway, next to the sunflower stumps.

There are other residents in the living room too, but Lawrence is speaking to no one in particular when he begins to talk about when he was a boy, about Small Street and his cousin Bertie and when everything around here was just fields. While Doris keeps her gaze on her television programme, Lawrence talks about the birds you saw then and the hedgerows that have gone. 'The skylark and thrush,' he says, 'the birds of the bush.'

Two of the other residents across the room have begun a conversation between themselves. Another one has closed his eyes. 'We were only children,' says Lawrence. 'Breathing English air, washed by the rivers, blest by suns of home.' Doris watches the rolling credits, while Lawrence quotes next from D.H. Lawrence, after whom he was named and whole passages of whose texts he knows by heart: 'It was a spring day, chill, with snatches of sunshine. Yellow celandines showed out from the hedge-bottoms . . .'

Someone is standing in the doorway—a young lady who is saying to him, 'What do you want?' She reminds him of the salesgirl in the department store who showed him the tray of engagement rings. 'Can I get you something?' she asks. And then he realises that it is the girl who comes down the corridor with a vacuum cleaner in the afternoon. The vacuum cleaner is the sort that has a happy face on the front; it wears a bowler hat. Smiling, it follows her around like a dog.

When they first told him about pat-a-dog day, Lawrence anticipated a golden retriever, like the puppy they had when Lewis was younger. It is a small dog though, not a puppy but a full-grown dog that will always be small. Lawrence has to reach almost to the floor to touch its coarse hair.

He knows that this is not craft day. Monday is craft day. The craft lady, who smells of vanilla and has a son in Afghanistan, has only recently been and will not come again until next week.

'We like to keep them busy,' said the manager, when Lewis first brought Lawrence here and asked about the programme of activities. There is a lot of singing. They have a microphone in the cupboard. Or they bring the kiddies from the infant school, line them up along the wall and get them to sing. Some of them sing their hearts out and some of them cry.

There is a man who comes with a keyboard once a month and does all the old tunes. He takes requests but he does not know Handel's *Messiah*, although he has said that he will have a go.

The girl has turned around and walked away.

Opening the cleaning cupboard, she wheels out the vacuum cleaner. Putting her head around the staff-room door, she says to the nurse who is in there, 'One of the men in the lounge is crying.'

'That will be Lawrence,' says the nurse, who is due a break and has just sat down.

'I think he wants something,' says the girl.

'He always wants something,' says the nurse. 'He spends half the night calling for a glass of water when he's already got one.'

The girl walks away again, pulling the vacuum cleaner down the corridor towards the lounge.

Lawrence sniffs at the air, detecting soup like an old sailor sensing a storm. Is he waiting, he wonders, for someone to come and take him to the dining room?

The girl comes back in and Lawrence half-expects to see in her hands a velvet-covered tray, a selection of rings, gold studded with precious stones, so that he can choose which one he wants, take it home in a little satin-lined box, a little bit of treasure in his pocket. She walks right up to him and says, 'What is it, Lawrence? Do you want a cup of tea?' She is holding the plug of the vacuum cleaner. She stoops to push it into a nearby socket, but she is waiting—her young face turned to him—for an answer.

'Yes, please,' says Lawrence.

'He wants a cup of tea,' says the girl, standing in the staffroom doorway with the happy Hoover at her heels.

'He always does,' says the nurse. 'He'll say yes to whatever you offer him.' Checking the time, putting aside the unfinished crossword, the nurse sighs and then stands up and goes to the kitchen to switch on the kettle.

It is not his bath day. Someone else is in the bath. He can hear a thin voice calling down the corridor, 'Are you coming to get me?'

He is not expecting the hairdresser, who comes every Friday to snip at the wispy white hairs around his ears.

'Is there anybody there?' calls that thin, high voice. 'Are you coming to get me?'

One of the nurses is approaching. It is the man nurse. He has long, curly hair and a man's voice. He wears shiny earrings and has a man's hands.

The man nurse, putting down the cup of tea he's brought, says, 'Do you want a blanket, Lawrence, over your legs?' When Lawrence says yes, please, the man nurse says, 'Do you want a coconut macaroon?'

When Lawrence says yes, please, the man nurse says, 'Do you want a dancing girl?' Lawrence, looking up into the man nurse's eyes, opens his mouth. The man nurse laughs and pats Lawrence's knee. 'Maybe tomorrow,' he says. 'Maybe tomorrow. Today, my friend, is pat-a-dog day.'

HE WANTS THE
FAMILY SILVER

WHEN HE OPENS his front door, Lewis, who has only had half a shandy, and not even that, is surprised to see his dog standing in the hallway. Then he realises that this cannot be his dog because his dog was lost half a lifetime ago, fifty-odd years ago. He wonders how long golden retrievers live for—not beyond their teens at least.

'Well,' says Lewis to this dog which is standing by the coat pegs smiling at him. 'Where have you come from?' He reaches into his pocket, looking for a treat, but the dog has turned around and is trotting down the hallway, heading into the living room. 'Are you hungry?' says Lewis to the dog's retreating backside. He follows, without stopping to take off his coat or his shoes. '*You*'d have had the vegetarian sausages,' he says. 'You'd have wolfed down whatever came your way, whatever fell on the floor.' He admires a good appetite, even if he himself does not eat much.

By the time he gets into the living room, the dog is already in the kitchen. 'Let's see what we've got for you,' says Lewis, as he comes to the kitchen doorway and stops, seeing the old man who is sitting at the kitchen table with one hand pressed to his chest. The man is wearing a yellow T-shirt with a logo on the front that makes Lewis think, 'Just Do It'.

Lewis—who has not had much in the way of lunch, who has just walked the half mile home from the pub, who has not had his usual rest on the second stair whilst taking off his shoes, and who, in addition, has, albeit briefly, had the shock of finding his dead dog alive in the hallway—pulls out the other chair and sits down. Reaching up to remove the hat from his head, he realises that he has left his hat in the pub, on the bar, next to the jar of pickled eggs. He feels instead a head of short hair that does not feel like his own. After taking a moment, he says to the man who is sitting in Edie's chair holding his heart, 'What are you doing in my house?'

The man, who has been looking at him, looks at him some more and then says, '*Your* house?'

'Yes,' replies Lewis. 'You are in my house. This is my kitchen. You are sitting in my wife's chair at my kitchen table. I thought for a moment that this was my dog.'

'This is *my* dog,' says the man.

'He was in the hallway when I came through the door,' says Lewis. 'He was smiling at me.'

'She always looks like she's smiling,' says the man. 'That's just how she is.'

What is he doing in my kitchen? wonders Lewis, and then, recalling a headline from the front page of the local paper, a report about thieves who have been operating in the vicinity, he thinks, *He's burgling me.*

His father used to worry about burglars. As soon as Lawrence left the house, he'd be imagining men, rough men, approaching his back door with crowbars and swag bags, looking to break in. This was after Lawrence had stopped teaching at the secondary school, when he had taken to getting a bus into town on market days so as to stand in the town centre, on the corner by the key-cutter, preaching. Lewis remembers the first time he saw him doing it, when, walking through town with a bunch of flowers in his hand, Lewis came across his father standing on the corner, speaking, at a mild volume, about the obscenity he had found in his books, his classics. He said it, thinks Lewis, as if it were something that had not been there before, as if something infectious had suddenly spread, like Dutch elm disease or ash dieback, through the volumes on his shelves. It was like when a boy at school had told everyone that he had walked in on his parents 'doing it' on the kitchen table, and it made Lewis, who had never seen or heard his parents doing anything in the least bit sexual, regard his own kitchen differently, warily. After this, when Lewis ate his breakfast cereal, he made sure that his spoon did not touch the tabletop, just in case.

He cannot remember now whether the flowers were for his mother or for Edie. Whenever he gave flowers to Edie, she would narrow her eyes and say to him, 'What have you done?' and he would say, 'Nothing.' She was only joking though; she knew, really, that he had never done anything.

After that first time, Lewis often saw his father standing outside the key-cutter, preaching about morality and decency. The Lord would come, his father said, and the world would end. 'We that are alive, that are left,' he said, rather quietly, to the people who walked past, 'shall be caught up in the clouds, to meet the Lord in the air. Then we will be with the Lord forever.' Those going by tried not to look at him. They did not even seem sure whether he was talking to them or just to himself.

Lawrence could not understand their lack of interest, when he, in the years after seeing Billy Graham and since being baptised, had come to long for the Rapture; he desired Christ's kingdom. He spoke to Lewis about the Great Disappointment of 1844, when thousands of people gave away their possessions in anticipation of a Rapture that never came. It seemed to Lewis that his father was sorry not to have been there, not to have been amongst them, as if that wealth of wanting was something desirable in itself, even though it all came to nothing in the end.

From time to time, there was a new prediction; the date of one Rapture after another was set, but then the day always came and went with the Rapture never materialising. When Lawrence watches the news, he is looking for earthquakes and floods; they are coming more frequently now, these signs that the Rapture is approaching. He has been looking forward to it not as the end but as the beginning of something. For years he has believed that it would come soon, but one year after another has been and gone and nothing has happened. He is surprised, in yet another New Year, to find that he is still here. He has begun to wonder if it is possible that he has just missed it, if it happened while he was sleeping, if he is just one of the many left behind. He is aware of further predictions of the date on which Jesus will return, predictions that the Rapture will take place within the next few years, by 2021 at the latest. In the meantime, he is desperate to hear from his Uncle Ted. There is still time. Lives are getting longer and longer. The nursing home has a computer that is mainly used for emailing and Skyping, but Lawrence googles, trying to find out if he might live to be a hundred, a hundred and one. He needs to start eating oily fish and avocados; he needs to start doing crossword puzzles, to drink more tea.

Lewis does believe in God. ('Or at least *something*,' he says, when having such conversations with people who do not. 'Don't you think there has to be something?' And he likes the idea of Jesus coming back, although he cannot envisage it, how it would happen. If he pictures it, he imagines a Byzantine Jesus, a figure from an ancient painting or a mosaic, with a golden glow all around him, not a real man who might belong to the twenty-first century.) He has never felt, though, what his father felt at Maine Road football stadium. He has never had that sort of world-shattering experience. He once wondered about going back there, if only to see a football match, but when he looked it up on the computer he found that it had been demolished years ago—like his father's house, which never was burgled, just bulldozed.

Lewis looks around his kitchen for things that might be missing. His Christmas fund is still in its jar on the shelf by the sink. He has not got much in there anyway; Christmas is a long way off. His wind-up radio, newly purchased with coupons he's been saving from the boxes his tea bags come in, is still on the windowsill, next to a vase of birthday flowers. Ruth has put something into the water to extend the life of the blooms. Vinegar, perhaps, or aspirin or sugar, all of which cut flowers apparently like.

He looks for a bag in which the man might have stashed the carriage clock that is kept in the living room. There is a full rucksack down on the floor by the man's feet. Perhaps he had almost finished and was on the brink of leaving when he was interrupted by a disturbance in his heart.

There is surely not that much to take, though, thinks Lewis. His computer is the sort that no one wants these days. It is big and old and grey; there is mostly empty space inside. His television would not be worth much. Perhaps the man expected to find Lewis's life savings hidden under the mattress. He came, supposes Lewis, thinking that there might be a safe full of valuable heirlooms at the back of the wardrobe. He wants the family silver. What he will find, in the top kitchen drawer, is a Post Office book for an account requiring thirty days' notice for withdrawals, and in the drawer below that, a decent set of stainless steel cutlery from Wilko.

There is, in fact, family silver but Lewis does not have it in his house. His sister boxed it up when they moved their father out of the house on Small Street and into his room at the nursing home. 'You can't take it with you,' she said to Lawrence, putting the cutlery canteen into the trunk of her car, along with the fine bone china and the crystal—wine glasses on long, thin stems, glasses for sherry and brandy— the wedding set that had always lived in the cabinet and had never been used for fear of breakage. 'You ought to wrap the glasses,' said Lawrence. 'You need to put sheets of newspaper in between the plates.' 'It will be fine,' said Lewis's sister, slamming the trunk, the breakables rattling. And then she drove this jangling kitchenware four hundred miles north to Aberdeen and then oversea, by ferry, to Shetland, where she has a house that none of them has ever visited. Lewis would find it hard to live where she does, what with the cold, and no supermarket, no bookshop, no HMV.

In a deep drawer in a spare room in the house on Small Street, there were hundreds of used envelopes with the top right-hand corner torn off, and, loose in a different drawer, hundreds of used stamps. Meaning to bag them up so as to gift them to Lewis, Lawrence reached into a plastic bag full of plastic bags that lived on a hook in the kitchen. Lewis came into the room and found his father staring at his hands as if he were Lady Macbeth. His hands were covered in what looked like small shards of broken glass, but there was no blood. And then Lewis realised that these were shards of transparent plastic, from the plastic bag full of plastic bags that must have disintegrated. Lawrence said, 'I thought plastic bags were supposed to last for hundreds of years.'

'Not when exposed to the light,' said Lewis.

The shards were dreadful to get off. They clung.

Lawrence could not take his Hi-fi, which was more than a metre wide, to the nursing home either, so Lewis bought him a CD player for his room. He needs some CDs. The only CDs the nursing home has are those ambient sounds they play on loop. They could do with a bit of Rachmaninov, thinks Lewis; they could do with a bit of AC/DC, a blast of noise slipped in amongst the dolphin song.

Lawrence could not take all his books with him and so Lewis has them, along with the stripy deckchairs.

It was soon after the bulldozing of the vacated house on Small Street that John came to stay. (Lewis missed the moment of demolition. When he looked, one morning, through the double glazing that muted the noise of the wrecking ball and the bulldozer, the house was just gone.)

A widower now, John came alone. Lewis had not seen him since that second and last visit to Manchester nearly fifteen years before. He was glad to see John but anxious to impress him or at least not to displease him. Before John arrived, Lewis put away the wine that had been visible in the kitchen—Edie's (*youthful, seductive*) New Zealand Merlot, her (*smooth, full-bodied*) Australian Shiraz. He weeded his garden and re-potted his azalea. Lewis offered John his spare room, Ruth's old bedroom. It was only when John had settled in, when his shirts were hanging up in the wardrobe and his pyjamas were underneath the pillow, that Lewis wondered whether he ought to have taken down the posters of the dead pop stars and dead films stars. Then John surprised him by doing an impressive pelvic gyration in front of the Elvis Presley poster, and later, over dinner, saying, 'I've always rather liked Cary Grant.'

It turned out that John no longer poured wine down the sink; he drank it, and enjoyed it. He accompanied Lewis to The Golden Fleece, this being a few years before Lewis's banishment. John proved to be popular and was quickly accepted by the locals. Sometimes, Ruth, who lived alone nearby, was invited along too. She occasionally talked about wanting children, but, at thirty ('and none of us getting any younger,' said Lewis) she was single, although Lewis understood that she had some sort of relationship going, something along the lines of a male pen pal.

John did not seem to be in any hurry to return to Manchester. He no longer had the animals to look after, he said, and what potatoes there were would grow just fine without him. Lewis enjoyed John's company. They were two old men in their retirement. In the daytime, they went for drives, parking up somewhere and trying to identify the birds and the aeroplanes that flew overhead. They went to vintage car shows, and airshows; they saw the Red Arrows looping the loop, leaving a vast, smoky O dispersing in the white sky. In the evening, they watched Cary Grant in old films or strolled to the pub for a nightcap.

It was on one such evening, as they were wandering home again and Lewis was looking up at the stars—'There's Venus,' he was about to say—that John asked Lewis for his blessing to marry Ruth. Lewis was entirely unprepared for this. Caught off guard, he walked along with his mouth open, no words coming out. Later, speaking privately to Ruth, he said, 'He's old enough to be your father. He's older than me. He's old enough to be your *grand*father.' But Ruth just shrugged, as if age were nothing. Lewis does not recall ever actually giving them his blessing, but they married anyway, and Lewis tries not to think too much about it, about this eighty-year-old man in his daughter's life. John still goes to The Golden Fleece; he goes there with Ruth, while Lewis looks after the boy, or John goes on his own and talks to his new friends, Lewis's old friends, the old boys. He is always sure to put in a good word for Lewis, who might, one day, find that he is able to go back.

HE WANTED TO LIVE IN AUSTRALIA

'I KNOW WHAT you want,' says the man, getting up and going over to Lewis's cupboards. The dog watches him with her tongue hanging out. The man opens and closes the cupboard doors, discovering sets of cups and saucers, some tinned and dried food, baking trays that have not been used for years, and a glass dish that he takes out and fills from the cold tap before putting it down too heavily on the stone-tiled floor. Lewis watches, the thought of breakage briefly raising his pulse.

'That's better, isn't it?' says the man as the dog sticks her nose into Edie's best pie dish and starts lapping. The dog has a barrel hanging from her collar, like a Saint Bernard's brandy barrel but smaller and plastic. It bangs rhythmically against the dish.

It comes to him suddenly. 'Sydney,' says Lewis (*with a 'y', like the capital of Australia*), and it is as if, by typing the name into Google, he has summoned Sydney, like a genie, like Candyman.

When he was a child, Lewis wanted to live in Australia. He wanted his family to move there so that he could live upside down. Everyone seems to know someone who has emigrated to the Antipodes. Lewis's great uncle went out there and never came home. They have lost touch with him; Ted does not answer—or does not receive—the letters that Lawrence sends, in which he always mentions his cousin Bertie. Lawrence and Bertie, born in the same year and raised together on Small Street, were drafted into the war at the same time. Returning home, both miraculously unscathed, they enjoyed rambling, hill-walking and hunting in the local countryside.

('Australia,' says Ruth's boy, 'is a million miles away.' No, says Lewis, not a million miles, that's further than the moon. But the boy is quite sure. 'It's a million miles away. It's further away than the moon.' MILL-*ee-on*, he says, making the number as big as he can, stretching it out. Or, as if that were not already far enough, 'A million and a hundred.')

It occurs to Lewis that Sydney's surprise when Lewis said to him 'You are in my house' suggests that Sydney cannot be here to see him. Sydney might not even have recognised him, might not have realised who he is.

'It's Lewis,' he says, touching his own chest, his own heart. 'Lewis Sullivan. We were at school together.'

'I know who you are, Lewie,' says Sydney.

Lewis has not been called Lewie since he was eighteen. He remembers that summer, when he and Sydney had finished school all except for their exams. Lewis spent much of his free time cycling around the village, where, one afternoon, he encountered Sydney, who was also out exploring on his bike. They rode along together for a while, without saying much, and then Sydney said, 'My dog had puppies. Do you want to come and see them?'

'Sure,' said Lewis, shrugging, as if he did not really mind one way or the other. He followed Sydney the half dozen miles to the nearby village that the locals call Nether, the pair of them freewheeling between fields of ripening winter barley, and acres of green grass that had not yet been built on, and the sky was so blue and so empty.

Sydney threw his bike down outside the only un-clad house in the terrace and greeted a girl coming by on a horse. She halted, pulling in the reins, and Sydney idly stroked the nose of her shifting, snorting mare while he spoke to this girl, who was their own age but who Lewis did not know. Lewis hung back, still straddling his bike, eating sweets from a bag he had on him, into which Sydney—reaching towards him but not quite enough so that Lewis was forced to come closer—stuck his hand, offering a sweet to the horse. The horse brought its nose forward, seeking out this treat with its flaring nostrils and its huge lips, and Lewis saw the enormous teeth in the whiskery mouth that nuzzled into the palm of Sydney's cupped hand.

'Do you want to give him one?' said Sydney, but Lewis could not bring himself to do it. Stepping away, he trod in some horse shit that he had not noticed or that had not been there before. He had to leave his shoes outside the door of Sydney's house and go inside in his socks.

The dog, a golden retriever, was in the kitchen, smiling at them as they walked through the door. It was wearing this collar with the little plastic barrel dangling from it. And there was a puppy, which Lewis picked up and it licked him on the lips. 'Do you want a puppy?' asked Sydney. Lewis laughed and the puppy licked him in the mouth. He put it down again. 'Seriously,' said Sydney, 'we've got rid of the rest. This is the last one. If you want it, take it.'

'I'll ask at home,' said Lewis.

Lewis, when he asked his father, was surprised to be told that he could have the puppy. He went over to Sydney's house again a few days later. Sydney was there, but his parents had taken the dogs out. Sydney took Lewis up to his room. There was a map of the world on Sydney's bedroom wall, with pins in places he wanted to visit. There was one in India, where he had been born, he said, in a British military hospital while his father was posted there. 'I'd like to go back,' he said. He talked about growing up on army bases, where he wasn't allowed to touch the walls of the houses in which they lived because they were only ever temporary residents and when they left they had to leave the houses just as they had found them. Lewis noticed after that that when Sydney moved around a house, even though these were permanent homes, he never touched the walls.

He did steal, though. He took strange liqueurs from his parents' drinks cabinet, and continental lagers from the fridge, Lewis mixing his with lemonade. Sydney's father also brewed his own beer. Some of the bottles exploded in the cupboard, the corks blasting out, and Lewis hoped to witness it happening again, or at least to see the aftermath, but he only saw the site cleaned up, the volatile beers moved out. He was not offered the explosive home brew.

Sydney stole one of his father's Woodbines too, lighting it and sharing it with Lewis, who put it to his lips but refrained from really smoking it, afraid of getting the smoke in his throat where it would burn, like loud music damaging the hairs inside your ears, making you deaf in old age.

The following week, Sydney brought the puppy over to Lewis's house on Small Street. He arrived in his father's Saab, sitting in the driver's seat and parking too far from the curb, watched from the living-room window by Lewis. When Lewis got to the door, his father had already opened it and was fussing over the puppy and christening him Old Yeller.

Lawrence invited Sydney into the house, taking him through to the living room. He expressed great interest in the fact that Sydney had been born abroad, that he had lived in so many different places and was keen on travelling. Lawrence had learnt all this from Lewis, who was surprised to discover that he had apparently said so much about Sydney to his father. Lawrence said to Sydney, 'Have you been to Australia?' and was disappointed when Sydney said that he had never been there. 'Are you going to go there someday though?' said Lawrence.

'Sure,' said Sydney.

'My uncle went out there,' said Lawrence. 'There are opportunities there. They're advertising for men. You can make a good living.'

'I want to go everywhere,' said Sydney. 'I want to see the Wonders of the World.'

'You're too late,' said Lawrence. 'Most of them have gone.' He moved towards the kitchen. 'Cup of tea?' he said. But Sydney, who had only just got there, was already keen to leave.

'Are you coming for a ride in the Saab?' he said to Lewis, who did not need asking twice. Leaving the new puppy with his father, Lewis followed Sydney outside.

They drove through the village with the windows down, the mother dog panting on the back seat. It was a glorious car, with a beautiful, rounded shape, and Lewis longed to sit behind the wheel himself. 'It's so cool,' he said, 'that your dad lets you drive his Saab.'

'He doesn't let me,' said Sydney, accelerating hard. 'He never lets the key out of his sight.'

'Then how come you're driving it now?' asked Lewis.

'I know where he keeps the spare key,' said Sydney.

They drove around the countryside for a while, 'like two old men,' said Lewis, 'like an old married couple out for a Sunday drive,' except that Sydney drove so fast, and on a particularly narrow lane nearly knocked a man off his bike.

Sydney drove them to Nether, pulling up outside his house. 'They're out,' he said as he parked. Letting the dog out of the car, he squatted down in front of her, took hold of her collar and opened up the brandy barrel. He put the spare car key inside and snapped the barrel shut.

They went into the house and up to Sydney's bedroom where they sat on the edge of Sydney's bed. Lewis had with him a book of his father's that he was carrying around and he showed it to Sydney. He was thinking about the part in it where Rupert proposes jiu-jitsu ('I'll show you what I can, if you like') and the two men end up wrestling, but Sydney was not greatly interested in D.H. Lawrence. Instead, Sydney showed Lewis the paperbacks he had stolen from a bookshop in town. Lewis read the epigraph in *The City and the Pillar*—'*But his wife looked back from behind him and she became a pillar of salt*'—and Sydney said, 'You can read it when I'm done with it.'

Sydney suggested breaking into the drinks cabinet and mixing up a couple of cocktails, but then they heard the ice cream van coming by and wondered if they'd prefer lollies. In the end they got neither. Sydney's parents came home unexpectedly while the boys were still sitting on the bed, while Lewis was still looking through the books, and Sydney's mother came upstairs, to Sydney's bedroom door, with home-made biscuits.

When Lewis said, 'Perhaps I should be going,' Sydney, lounging on the bed, said, 'Don't go yet.' They talked some more and Sydney read Lewis a short story he had recently written, and then, though Lewis lingered, Sydney moved towards the door.

On the doorstep, Sydney's father asked what Lewis was planning to do with himself now. Lewis mentioned a trip to Manchester that his father and he were going to take, and then, at the end of the summer, he would be going away to university.

'Good,' said Sydney's father.

Sydney had wanted to do his national service in the air force; he had wanted to fly aeroplanes, to go abroad, but by the time he came of age, national service had come to an end. His parents wanted him to join up anyway. 'They'll make a man of you,' his father had said, his gaze sliding from Sydney to Lewis, whose hair had already begun to grow over his ears.

Lewis, who had been banking on a lift, walked home. When he got there, he looked for the puppy but could not find him anywhere. He said to his father, 'Where's the puppy?'

His father, looking up from his reading, said, 'Old Yeller? I let him into the garden.'

They went out there, but there was no puppy in the garden. They walked up and down the road and looked over the gate into the field but the puppy was nowhere to be seen. Lewis kept expecting the puppy to return, to be in the garden the next time he looked, but the garden remained empty. He would have to come back when he wanted his breakfast, thought Lewis, but the puppy never materialised. On a few occasions during that week, the doorbell rang, and Lewis, going to the window, hoped that it would turn out to be a neighbour holding the wriggling puppy, but each time it was Sydney. Lewis had stomach cramps all week and wasn't well enough to go out with Sydney or even to stand on the doorstep and speak to him. He went to bed. Then Lewis and his father went to Manchester and by the time they returned, Sydney had gone and his parents seemed unable or unwilling to say exactly where to, or to supply his new address. Lewis never had been loaned *The City and the Pillar*. He went to the bookshop in town but could not bring himself to ask for it.

He ate too many ice lollies that summer. He kept hearing the ice cream van coming, and going outside to meet it. He got frozen insides and his father said, 'No wonder you got stomach cramps.'

Lewis went south to university without knowing what Sydney would end up doing, but every time a plane went overhead, Lewis stopped and looked up, thinking of Sydney.

At Christmas, Lewis came home and cycled straight over to Sydney's house wearing tinsel as a scarf, but Sydney's father stood in the doorway and said that Sydney was not there.

Occasionally, in the years that followed, Lewis would hear rumours that Sydney was coming back, but either the rumours were wrong or Lewis kept missing him. The next time Lewis saw him, Sydney was sitting on the hood of a car with his shirt off and Lewis was on his way to get married.

'Why are you sitting at my kitchen table?' asks Lewis.

'I had a pain,' says Sydney, 'in my heart. I had to sit down.'

'But what are you doing in my house?'

'I didn't know it was your house.'

Yes, thinks Lewis, who was still living on Small Street when he knew Sydney. And the dog—even if it had come back after all this time, after four or five dog lifetimes—would not have come to this house, it would have gone to Small Street and found itself standing in a parking lot.

Lewis says to Sydney, 'How did you get in?'

'Your back door was unlocked,' says Sydney, and Lewis, looking, can see that the bolt is not across. He must have forgotten to bolt it after going to the bin. It must have been unlocked all night. Sydney must have let himself in while Lewis was having his lunch at the pub. Perhaps while he was rejecting the sausages, eyeing the Goldschläger man, choosing a pickled egg, Sydney was here.

Lewis says to Sydney now, 'Have you ever had Goldschläger?'

'I've tried it,' says Sydney. 'You've got to try these things, haven't you?'

Lewis nods, but he says, even as he is nodding, 'I never have.'

He is missing his glasses, clarity of vision. He stands and wanders over to the units, opening a drawer and rummaging through unused gadgets, looking for his spare pair. He finds the case but there are no glasses inside.

'Pop the kettle on while you're up,' says Sydney.

Lewis puts it on, takes a couple of teacups from the cupboard and gets out the cake tin. Inside, he discovers a walnut cake that he has not yet cut into but which is starting to go stale. 'Shall we have some cake?' he asks.

'Go for it,' says Sydney.

Lewis delivers the cups of tea to the table, and then two small plates of cake. He has put little forks on the plates but Sydney eats with his fingers, not waiting to swallow one bite before taking another, making sounds of pleasure all the while. Lewis finds himself doing the same, grunting happily with each mouthful of cake, each sip of tea.

Sydney, finishing his slice, licks his fingers and tastes his tea. Pulling a face, he gets up and goes over the counter, opens up the sugar caddy and dips in his spoon.

As Sydney comes back to the table, he touches the back of Lewis's neck. 'Have you had that looked at?' he asks. Lewis brings his hand up to the soft, brown lump newly exposed at the nape, between his hairline and his collar. He cannot tell if the lump is getting bigger.

'I'm having it cut out,' says Lewis. 'I've got an appointment at the surgery this afternoon.'

'I'd offer to give you a lift,' says Sydney, 'but I was planning on waiting for Ruth.'

Lewis feels a jolt, much like when Ruth says 'Jesus' or 'Christ' under her breath.

'Ruth?' he says. 'My Ruth?'

Sydney takes a loose cigarette out of his pocket. He does not ask Lewis whether he may smoke in the house, in the kitchen; he does not ask for an ashtray. He puts the cigarette between his lips. Just as Lewis is realising that something is not quite right, Sydney holds the cigarette out for him to see. 'It's an electronic one,' says Sydney. He looks at it in a way that makes Lewis think of a spoonful of cold soup. Sydney puts the electronic cigarette in his mouth again and draws, making the end light up. He sighs and puts it away. 'She's not expecting me.'

'Ruth doesn't live here,' says Lewis. 'She hasn't lived here for years.' For a fleeting moment, Sydney looks sufficiently confused that Lewis almost reaches out to cover Sydney's trembling hand with his own.

'She comes here, though,' says Sydney.

'She won't come today,' says Lewis. He touches the back of his neck again, his growth, and looks at his bare wrist. 'What time is it?' he asks. When Sydney tells him, Lewis says, 'Time's marching on.' He will have to go soon. 'How do you know my Ruth?' he asks.

'We've never met,' says Sydney. 'We've been communicating.'

'She gave you this address?'

'No.'

'Well then, why did you come here?'

'You've got my book,' says Sydney. He is looking at the work surface, at a Bliss Tempest book that Ruth must have left out on the side.

'What?' says Lewis, following his gaze. 'No, that's *my* book.'

When Lewis turns back, he sees Sydney slumped, as if he has fainted, or, he thinks, it is his heart. Sydney's head is hanging down near the corner of the table. Lewis reaches out and is just about to touch him when he sees that Sydney is only bending down, fetching something out of his rucksack. Taking out a tall carton with a colourful Oriental design on a gold background, Sydney says, 'I brought some sake for Ruth.'

'I've never had sake,' says Lewis.

'What you really want,' says Sydney, 'is to have it in Tokyo, in a bar, with snacks—pickles and fish.' Putting the carton down on the kitchen table, he mentions the pickled herring eaten with beer in Germany and Scandinavia, and Thailand's painfully hot bar snacks, and Lewis thinks enviously of all those flights.

'I've never flown,' he says.

'It's safer than driving,' says Sydney. 'It's safer than crossing the road.'

'I'm not afraid of flying,' says Lewis. 'It's just something I've never done.' He has no idea why. He has been inside his nearest airport; he has been in the departure hall, where the first thing you see is a sign for the prayer room, and a picture of a little man down on his knees. He has seen the destinations on the information screens, the queues of people in front of the desks where passports are checked, boarding cards are issued and luggage is weighed. He just hasn't ever been the one going anywhere.

'You're most likely to be injured at home,' says Sydney. 'You're most likely to be harmed or killed by someone you know. You're safest of all in the air.'

'I believe you,' says Lewis, 'although at some point you would have to come down.'

Lewis reaches into the pocket of his coat and takes out a small paper bag. Opening it up, he holds it out to Sydney, who looks inside and extracts a jelly baby. The dog comes to the table, and Lewis gives her a sweet too. 'You're getting fat,' says Sydney, and Lewis can't tell if Sydney is talking to him or to the dog.

When Lewis saw the 'screaming jelly baby' experiment executed in the chemistry laboratory, he had been teaching for more than forty years and was approaching retirement, but as he watched the demonstration—his colleague, in a white coat and safety goggles, melting potassium chlorate in a boiling tube over a Bunsen burner, dropping in a jelly baby that burst into flames and began to howl—he wondered for the first time whether he ought to have chosen something other than Religious Studies, something more dramatic. In truth, though, Lewis could not have handled a career as a high-school chemistry teacher. He found the potential for accidents unnerving—the regular shattering of glass slides and test tubes, the explosions caused by adolescents not reading instructions, the constant smell of gas.

'Did you join the RAF?' asks Lewis.

Sydney looks puzzled. 'No,' he says.

'You wanted to be a writer too.'

'I did,' says Sydney.

Lewis glances at Sydney's watch, which he cannot read. 'I'll have to go in a minute,' he says. 'It's a bit of a walk to the surgery.'

'I'll take you,' says Sydney. 'I've got the car outside.'

Lewis, whose knee hurts when he walks, is quick to accept Sydney's offer.

Sydney stands, putting on his coat and shouldering his rucksack. Lewis is still wearing his coat and shoes from before. As he follows Sydney and his dog out of the kitchen, Lewis feels strangely as if he has only been visiting, as if he does not really belong here at all.

HE WANTS A
SECOND CHANCE

LAWRENCE WRITES HIS letters with a dip pen that once belonged to his Uncle Ted. He still has the original ink bottle, with a little purple ink left inside it. The ink, when it dries on the page, is the same shade as the interior walls of the nursing home. Lawrence thinks he could write all over the walls with this pen and no one would even know. He could say the things he would rather not say to anyone's face. *Your dog*, he would write, *is too small*. And: *I'm not all that fond of the processed meat*. And: *You don't always come when I call*. He could write these messages in big capital letters, like shouting that no one would hear. He would write to the craft lady: *I've always liked the way you smell*. It would be like using invisible ink.

He once sent a girl a Valentine's Day card. He put it boldly through her letterbox with his name inside, written in lemon juice. She never mentioned it. On some occasion after that, Lawrence did something he shouldn't have done (he does not remember now what it was; perhaps he had taken someone's sweets) and it occurred to him that he could make his confession in that same way, in writing, with his homemade invisible ink. That way, he reckoned, if he died in the night, he would get into heaven but without the grown-ups ever needing to know what he had done. (Perhaps it was that time he took some jam without asking, getting into the pantry and sticking his fingers right into the jar.) His mother, though, lit a match and held it close to the surface of his white sheet of paper, revealing his secret writing with the flame, and sent him to his father to be punished as his father saw fit. (What crime had he committed? He might have cut off his sister's doll's hair. It would be something like this, something small and quick but irreversible.)

His handwriting is good; he is careful with the pen. He dots his 'i's and crosses his 't's and the loops beneath his 'g's and 'j's and 'y's are small and neat. At school, he was naturally inclined to write with his left hand but that was soon forced out of him and instead he learnt to manage with his right. A poem he transcribed using his best calligraphy won him a certificate, presented in assembly, after which his Uncle Ted gave him the pen. He sat Lawrence down at his kitchen table and asked him to demonstrate his fine penmanship. He winced to see how Lawrence pressed the nib of this lovely pen against the paper, bearing down on it so hard that it splayed, and splayed to such an extent that the inked line split. The solid white line of bare paper left down the middle was like the line on the road that means you must not cross it. 'Don't press so hard,' said his Uncle Ted. 'You'll damage the nib.' The forcefulness of Lawrence's full stops made him gasp as if he himself had been stabbed with the nib. Lawrence wondered whether his Uncle Ted regretted, even then, saying that he could take the pen. Perhaps he would have liked to say, 'I'm afraid I've changed my mind. This pen is very valuable to me and I do not think you are exhibiting sufficient care. I do not want to give it to you after all. I do not want to put it into your hands.' But he did not say that. He did query the granting of the certificate, as if it were like a qualification, a licence, paperwork for a skill that Lawrence did not yet seem to have mastered. He still gave Lawrence the precious pen though, and Lawrence tried to press more lightly on the paper, striving to write well with his Uncle Ted's pen in his right hand, always hoping for another certificate. Even when his Uncle Ted went away, he did not ask for his pen back; he did not speak to Lawrence at all.

Even now, in his nineties, in the twenty-first century, when no one would care or especially notice if Lawrence wrote with his left hand, he still uses his right. No one would bother if he pressed down too hard, but if anything he does not press hard enough—the marks he makes are light, and shaky, his hand unable to hold the pen quite as steady as he would like. He uses a proper writing pad, containing forty sheets of nice, watermarked paper, and a guiding sheet that he puts underneath, the thick black lines keeping him straight.

He sends his opinions to the local newspaper, in letters alerting people to the dangers facing society, threats to the community, vandalism and graffiti in the streets, the damage to the bus shelter and the amendment of street signs. *SMELL STREET*. His most recent letters were intended to discourage people from visiting the medium who was coming—according to the nurses, according to the notices on the telephone poles and the gossip at the church—to the function room of the nearby pub, to commune with the dead. Lawrence signs his letters 'Mr L. Sullivan'. Lewis wishes he would not. 'What if people think it's me?' he asks. 'What if people think I'm the one complaining and saying these things?'

Lawrence's letters are never printed anyway.

After Lawrence's third and final missive about the medium, the nursing home staff decided to take the residents along to this event, this evening of communication with the spirits of the dead, as a treat. The craft lady expressed an interest in joining them, which left Lawrence conflicted. He pictured the two of them strolling up the road arm in arm, the craft lady's vanilla scent on the night air. But, he said, he would not be going, because that sort of thing—summoning the dead—was just not right. At worst it was toying with the devil and at best it was a con.

'But have you ever been to one of these evenings?' the craft lady said. 'It might not be like you're thinking it will be.' She'd been to one, she told him. She'd expected the room to be dark, 'like how you'd turn off the lights to do a Ouija board. But they kept the lights on,' she said, and more than anything else, it made her believe in heaven; it made her believe that we go to heaven when we die and that our loved ones are waiting there for us.

And so, on the evening of the event, the craft lady helped Lawrence out of the minibus and into the pub, and then up to the function room whose plastic chairs were set out in rows. She sat beside him and held his hand. 'See?' she said. 'They keep the lights on.'

When everyone was seated, the house lights were lowered. 'Oh,' said Lawrence, and the craft lady squeezed his hand. A young man in a plain shirt walked onto the stage. He was going to point out the exit, thought Lawrence; he was going to tell them about the fire assembly point and the happy hour deal at the bar. But this, it turned out, was the medium. Lawrence had been expecting a woman, robes, a bit of shimmer. The audience, sitting in the dim half of the room, gazed expectantly towards the spotlight, towards this man who was preparing to bring messages through from the other side. Lawrence looked around at the rest of his party. Even the ones who had said that they did not believe in this sort of thing were waiting, he reckoned, to hear their name called out or the name of someone they had lost.

'I have a Mary,' said the man. 'Can anyone claim Mary?'

And he said, 'I'm getting the scent of roses. Who liked roses?'

He strode across the room with his fingers pressed to his temples as if his head ached. 'There's a lady here,' he said, 'who wants to say she's sorry. Who's David?'

It was all such nonsense, thought Lawrence.

'I'm seeing bluebells.'

The craft lady had let go of Lawrence's hand so that she could eat the crisps she had got from the bar. He couldn't smell her perfume; he could just smell smoky bacon.

Much later, Lawrence wondered about the bluebells, but by then he was back at the nursing home, alone in his bedroom, and the medium was long gone.

He writes, as well, to his Uncle Ted. *Dear Uncle Ted*, he writes, even though Ted did not like Lawrence to call him 'Uncle' once Lawrence was no longer a child. 'Call me Ted,' he had said, before the accident, after which he did not say it again.

Lawrence writes every month. Each letter says much the same thing as the last one. His Uncle Ted has never written back. Lawrence worries that if his

Uncle Ted is not receiving these letters, then should his Uncle Ted want to contact him, he would not know how. He would not know that the houses on Small Street are gone. Lawrence imagines letters from his Uncle Ted delivered to the supermarket parking lot, blown against windshields and binned, or blown into puddles, ground beneath tires.

I am still in the village, he writes, *although where we lived on Small Street is a parking lot now.* He does not mention his children, both of them retired now, with children of their own, and even grandchildren.

I want you to know, he writes, *that I am sincerely sorry about what happened in the woods. I hope you know that I loved Bertie like a brother. I wish I had woken up that morning and found that it was raining or foggy so that we could not go out hunting, or that we had finished hunting half an hour earlier, when Bertie suggested stopping and coming home for tea, or that I had not taken that final shot at what I thought was something else, an animal in the bushes, or at least that I had missed his heart.*

He does not say, *He bled so much. I was kneeling beside him, trying to stop the blood coming out. When I finally stood up, I was like Lady Macbeth.*

I hope you are well, he says, *and I look forward to your reply.* He ensures that his postal address is on the letter, and then he signs it, folds it, puts it in an envelope and sends it to Australia. He does not know his Uncle Ted's address but sends his letters care of the post office. He does not know which city or town his Uncle

Ted might be in, so he spreads the letters around. He has sent them to Sydney, Melbourne, Brisbane and Perth; to Adelaide, Wollongong, Townsville and Cairns; to Darwin, Toowoomba, Ballarat and Bendigo; to Canberra, Orange, Coffs Harbour and Broken Hill; to Albany and Albury and Bunbury; to Shepparton, Whyalla, Mount Isa and Mackay; to Rockhampton, Bundaberg, Port Hedland and Port Lincoln; to Maryborough and Alice Springs; to Tamworth and Wagga Wagga. 'Where are we sending it this time?' asks the nurse. 'Outer Mongolia? Timbuktu?'

Lewis says—every month, when Lawrence mentions that he has written his letter—that he very much doubts that Ted is still alive, but Lawrence cites people who have lived to be a hundred and fifteen, a hundred and sixteen. 'A woman in France,' says Lawrence, 'lived to be a hundred and twenty-two.'

Ruth brought him some airmail stationery, the sort where one sheet is both paper and envelope, the blue page thin and delicate like the pressed petals of the bluebells that grow in the woods. Lawrence prefers to use the proper, heavier writing paper, the good, heavy envelopes. It costs him more.

He watches the nurse walk away with his letter. It is possible, he thinks, that his Uncle Ted receives them all, that every letter Lawrence sends him finds him in the end. He imagines them dropping through his Uncle Ted's letterbox, one after another, wherever he is. He puts away his writing pad, puts the lid back on the bottle of ink and looks again at his pen. He wonders whether his Uncle Ted, if he saw the handwriting on the front of the envelope, would recognise the shade of the ink, the thickness of the line, the characteristics of his old pen, and he thinks, then, of a Stephen King novel that Edie once mentioned reading, in which a man is bludgeoned to death with his own severed arm.

HE WANTS TO
BE SEEN

BEFORE LEAVING THE house for his appointment at the surgery, Lewis takes his broken glasses out of his coat pocket and puts them down on the table in the hallway, to remind himself to get them mended. Also on the table is an ill-fitting dental plate that he needs to show to his dentist. The table resembles a small shrine to an old man, or an altar bearing sacrificial offerings so that the gods will look upon him kindly.

Lewis walks with Sydney to the yellow car that is parked by the curb, in the same space Ruth was occupying earlier. Patting the roof, he says to Sydney, 'It's lasted well.'

'It's still going,' agrees Sydney, holding the passenger door open for Lewis, who lowers himself into the front seat, the leather upholstery creaking.

Sydney, getting into the driver's seat, says, 'So you read Bliss Tempest?'

'No,' says Lewis. 'It's not my sort of thing.'

'How do you know,' says Sydney, 'if you've never read it?' It is the sort of thing they say to the boy when he is looking dubiously at a vegetable: *How do you know, if you've never tried it?*

Sydney starts the engine and the hula girl on the dashboard starts to shake. Pulling away from the curb without looking, Sydney forces an oncoming Ford to swerve into the far lane, the driver leaning on the horn. 'Jesus fucking Christ,' says Sydney. The blasphemy stabs into Lewis like the sharpened tip of a pencil into bared skin. He can feel himself blushing. Sydney doesn't even tap the brake but keeps on going, the long, reproachful honk of the Ford's horn still echoing off the fronts of the houses.

Lewis is sitting uncomfortably. There is a big box of tapes in the footwell on the passenger side, forcing his legs towards Sydney, and the springs have gone in his seat. The dog is standing on the back seat, panting into Lewis's ear. There is hot dog breath on Lewis's neck, and something dribbling down inside his collar, saliva from the tip of the dog's huge tongue.

They are speeding when they pass the church that Lewis attends with his father every Sunday. (It is not the sort of church that has grotesques, cold stone walls, stone pillars and pews and that is older than anyone alive. It looks like a house with a double-glazed porch. It has padded chairs that can be rearranged or stacked and put away so that the room can be used for other things.) 'This is a thirty,' says Lewis, even though they are going too fast for Sydney to have mistaken the zone for a forty. They are bearing down on the Ford. Lewis can see a sign in the rear window. He can't make out the words but it is the sort that says 'BABY ON BOARD'. Sydney's eyes are narrowed. 'Sydney,' says Lewis. He is bracing for impact when the Ford takes a turn without indicating, pulling off the main road so suddenly that its back wheels skid, leaving black tire tracks at the junction. Sydney glares at the back of the Ford as he shoots by. His hands are tight around the steering wheel, like hands rigid from a bike ride in cold weather. That's something Lewis has not experienced since he was a boy.

Sydney slows the car down. Lewis is worried that Sydney will turn the car around and go back to the junction in pursuit of the Ford. But instead, doing no more than thirty past a travel agency, Sydney turns his head to look at the posters in the window, the adverts for distant places. He says to Lewis, 'Have you been to the Caribbean?'

'No,' says Lewis.

'Barbados is sinking.' He mentions islands that Lewis has never been to that are already long gone.

They pass a new block of flats hung with a huge banner that says, in capital letters three feet high, 'LIVE WITH FRIENDS OR ON YOUR OWN'. It sounds to Lewis like a threat, an ultimatum.

Lewis says to Sydney, 'Do you live on your own?'

'Yes,' says Sydney.

When Sydney offers nothing more, Lewis says, 'Me too. Ruth's nearby though, and Dad's in the nursing home. I see him on Sundays. They do activities and he has a nice room. He's got a CD player so he can play his own music. He wants a copy of Handel's *Messiah*—he asked me months ago but I haven't been into town to get it.' He has been meaning to go to the HMV that he's seen where What Everyone Wants used to be before that went into administration. 'I need to go to HMV,' he says.

'The HMV's gone,' says Sydney. 'The sign's still up but the shop's been gutted.'

They drive past the old Hovis advert painted on the side of a building, at the end of a terrace. The paint is flaky and faded now but the message that has been there since he was a boy—HOVIS FOR TEA—is still faintly visible.

'You could order it online,' says Sydney. Lewis is anxious, though, about buying things online. He is worried that when he has typed in the numbers from his debit card, he will find all the money drained from his account; he will wake up in the morning and his savings will be gone, into the pockets of strangers.

Sydney pulls into the surgery parking lot and finds a free space. 'I'll wait in the car,' he says.

Lewis climbs out of the passenger seat and heads for the entrance, the automatic doors. Inside, he registers his arrival on the touch screen and takes a seat in the waiting room. He reaches for a magazine before remembering that he does not have his glasses. The magazine print is too small for him to make out without them. He expects, anyway, that he will soon be called. He looks around at the other waiting patients, and then up at the digital information screen above the reception desk. It says, in huge letters, 'YOU WILL NOT BE SEEN!!'

They are playing 'Greensleeves' on loop, an instrumental version, the same music you hear when you are on hold. The information screen emits a beep from time to time and all heads turn to look, and then someone stands and leaves the waiting area. He finds himself looking expectantly at the screen even when there is no beep.

It says, 'DO YOU WANT TO STOP?'

He does not like waiting rooms. He does not like these shiny, plastic chairs, the rows of failing bodies, the big, slow clock. He does not like waiting at the dentist's either, wondering if he is about to lose another tooth. They don't put you to sleep; they pull them out while you are wide awake.

The walls here are the colour of honey-and-lemon Strepsils. He once became addicted to Strepsils. He could get through a strip of twelve in an hour when the maximum dosage was one lozenge, dissolved slowly in the mouth, every two to three hours, and no more than twelve in a day. He'd had to hide the empty packaging from Edie—she'd have seen it, the unusual amount of it, in the kitchen bin. Sharing it out between the various household waste baskets would have been equally risky. She would have come to him, holding the recently discarded packets, asking him if his cough had not yet gone. Instead, he put the blister packs and little cardboard boxes in his coat pocket and dropped them into a public bin on his way to work. He tried to wean himself off them, these lozenges that were like sweets but with a little kick, that were yellow with an S on the front, slightly raised so that he could feel it with his tongue. He cut down to half a strip a day and then only a few lozenges and then just one in the morning, but he always went back onto them, especially after a lunchtime shandy. In the end, he bought a tin of lemon drops and whenever he wants a Strepsil he has a lemon drop or a lemon sherbet or a jelly baby instead, although it is not really the same.

'IF YOU DO NOT HAVE A PRE-BOOKED APPOINTMENT,' says the digital information screen.

After fifteen minutes, Lewis approaches the reception desk and asks why he has not been called. 'You'll be called when it's your turn,' says the receptionist.

Lewis tells her how long he has been waiting but he gets no reply. She is holding a phone to her ear although she does not seem to be having a conversation with anyone on the other end. He returns to his seat.

There is a woman sitting opposite him. She is eating Golden Wonder crisps from a family pack and reading a self-help book, one of half a dozen, a pile from the library. Another woman, eyeing these books, says to her, 'Those should keep you busy!'

'I love my books,' says the Golden Wonder woman, as, with a greasy, salted finger, she folds down a corner of her borrowed book.

Lewis looks up at the information screen ('DO YOU SMOKE?' it says) and then at the clock. He wonders whether Sydney is still outside in his car, whether he has waited for him. Lewis has been waiting in here for twenty minutes. He thinks he has waited long enough. He wants someone to call his name. They don't do that any more though. They put the names up on the screen. Lewis wants it to be his turn; he wants to be seen.

There is a beep, and when Lewis looks up he sees his name and a room number displayed. He leaves his uncomfortable, slippery chair and goes off to find the right room.

A nurse is standing at a steel trolley, arranging surgical tools on a steel tray. She tells Lewis where to sit and he sits. He thinks of the school nurse, to whom boys went with trophies of their daring, their derring-do—their sprained ankles, their fractured wrists, their gashes that might require stitches. Lewis never had cause to see the school nurse. He never needed to be taken to Accident and Emergency. He was never the centre of any drama. He has never broken anything or even had a sprain. He has never had stitches. His temperature has never been especially high. Now, though, he is sitting in a chair in the middle of the treatment room, waiting to be seen to. He is going to have an operation, and when he leaves, he will have stitches.

The nurse tucks a paper towel into the collar of Lewis's shirt. 'Hopefully there won't be too much blood,' she says, tucking in a second sheet as well.

The doctor breezes in. 'How's your father?' he says.

Lewis, thrown by the question, hesitates. He has opened his mouth and is on the verge of replying when the nurse interrupts.

'He's getting worse,' she says.

The doctor, standing behind Lewis, inspects the questionable mole, picks up a syringe and pokes the needle into the site, injecting the anaesthetic.

'He can't cope with the stairs any more.'

Lewis is aware of the doctor selecting a scalpel, and that a hole is being made in him, although he can't feel a thing.

'He can't manage the dog.'

He can feel the doctor's rounded stomach pressing against him, the slight shift and rise and fall of it against his back. He can hear the doctor breathing.

'It's too big for him, it's huge. He expects me to have it but I don't want it. I'd have it put down.'

'We always send these things off, just to make sure they're normal,' says the doctor, putting the growth, this little bit of Lewis, into a plastic pot for sending away. He looks at Lewis over his glasses. 'I trust it will be, but we'll send it anyway, just to make sure. You'll only hear from us if there's anything wrong.'

The nurse cleans some blood from Lewis's neck and removes the protective paper towels. It seems to be time for him to stand up and leave. At the door, he turns to thank the doctor, who has already left through another door. Lewis says to the nurse, 'I'll take your father's dog,' and the nurse laughs and turns away to attend to the instruments and the pots.

It is only when Lewis has let himself out, when the door has closed behind him, that he wonders whether the doctor, having removed the growth, remembered the stitches. He did not feel the needle going in to sew him up. He did not feel the tug of brightly coloured thread closing the wound. And even imagining that happening, he feels not so much like one of the more daring boys at school on a trip to Accident and Emergency, but instead like a teddy that needs to be darned where he has worn thin.

HE WANTS THE
MESSIAH

LEWIS WALKS BACK through the Strepsil-yellow waiting room, exiting through the automatic doors. He
half-expects to find Sydney gone and his knee aches at
the thought of the walk home.

But the Saab is parked right where it was. Sydney
is out of the car, sitting on the hood, just as he once
sat under the jubilee bunting except that then he had
his shirt off in the sunshine and now he is wearing a
gabardine coat and his hands look a little bit blue in
the last of the winter daylight.

'Does it hurt?' says Sydney, putting away his electronic cigarette and lowering himself off the hood.

'I can hardly feel it,' says Lewis. He opens the door
on the passenger side and gets in.

Sydney climbs into the driver's seat and leans over,
inspecting the back of Lewis's neck. 'Nice job,' he says.

'Are there stitches?' asks Lewis.

'There's a stitch,' says Sydney.

Holding on to the back of Lewis's seat with one hand, Sydney leans forward, reaching into the box of tapes in the footwell, rummaging through the contents. Lewis turns his head to the window. He can sense the approach of spring. In the coming months, the country air will fill with pollen. His eyes will redden and start to water; his nose will run. He never got hay fever when he was a boy; it came on later. If he was ever going to run through a meadow, knee deep in grasses and wild flowers, he ought to have done it while he was young, when he had the chance.

He can feel Sydney's cold fingers touching the back of his neck, but when he turns his head he sees that Sydney has both his hands in the box of tapes now and it is not Sydney but the dog that is touching him, her wet nose against the back of his neck, and then a wet tongue right where the wound is.

Sydney, sitting up again, puts a tape into Lewis's hands. 'That's for your dad,' he says. When Lewis looks at it blankly, Sydney says, 'That's the recording he wants, the *Messiah* he asked you to get for him.'

'Ah,' says Lewis. 'Thank you. I'll give it to him on Sunday.'

'Let's go and see him now,' says Sydney, choosing another tape to put into the car's tape deck.

'He won't be expecting visitors today,' says Lewis, but Sydney is already heading for the exit with his turn signal flashing. When he turns in the direction of the nursing home, it is with the Rolling Stones blasting from his speakers so loudly that, despite the windows being up, people turn and stare.

The nursing home has an unnecessarily large parking lot at the front. All this empty tarmac, thinks Lewis, and no garden. Sydney parks the Saab in the middle of a vacant row of marked-out spaces. They get out and go to the front door, where Lewis enters the four-digit code that keeps the residents safe.

There is a woman standing just inside the entrance hall. She reaches for them as they enter. 'I want to go home,' she says, holding on to their sleeves, their wrists. She has her hair in two long plaits and Lewis thinks of Dorothy from *The Wizard of Oz*, grown old, and then he thinks of his grandparents' beach hut even though it was not, of course, lifted into the heavens and flown to Oz but was smashed to bits right there on the beach. Lewis did not see it happen; he only saw the space where it had stood.

Sydney pulls away from the woman but she holds Lewis back. 'You don't regret what you've done,' she says. 'You'll regret what you haven't done.' Lewis looks at her, not knowing what to say, and then he too pulls away, pursuing Sydney.

Lewis is used to coming here on a Sunday to escort his father to church. Entering the lounge now, Lewis half-expects to be going to church next. He notices his unpolished shoes. He pats absentmindedly at his pocket, checking for change that he does not have on him, looking for something for the collection plate.

His father is sitting very upright in his chair. He is preaching. 'Cunt,' he says. Gripping his knees, he says, 'Balls.' There is an untouched cup of tea at his elbow. 'Shit and arse,' he says.

Lewis pulls up a couple of visitors' chairs, taking one from near Doris whose son will not arrive until teatime. He places the chairs in front of his father, who looks up and greets Lewis pleasantly enough but not by name, so that Lewis cannot tell whether his father knows who he is. His father also turns to Sydney and, frowning, narrowing his eyes, stares hard at him.

'We've brought you that *Messiah* you wanted,' says Sydney, looking at Lewis, who holds out the tape.

Lawrence, looking at it, says, 'I don't have a cassette player.'

'Oh,' says Lewis, 'that's right.'

Lawrence turns and looks again at his other visitor.

'Do you remember Sydney?' asks Lewis.

'You were telling me about your uncle,' says Sydney. 'The one who went to Australia.'

'Oh yes,' says Lawrence, brightening up. 'There were opportunities there. They were advertising for men. You could make a good living. I've never been.'

Lewis is about to change the subject, to ask his father what he had for his lunch, but Sydney begins to speak about Australia, describing for Lawrence the Australian birdlife: the yellow figbird, the golden whistler. It is the males, he says, that have the yellow throats, the golden underparts; the females are drab, grey and brown. And while he speaks, Lawrence, with his feet amongst the enormous flowers on the carpet, is as rapt as if he were actually there, at the edge of the rainforest, gazing up into the trees, towards the sky.

'You've got a cup of tea here, Dad,' says Lewis. 'Shall I pass it to you?'

'Yes, please,' says Lawrence.

Lewis picks it up by the saucer and hands it to Lawrence, who places it on his lap but does not drink it. He looks at the coconut macaroon that is in his saucer but he does not eat it.

'Oh,' he says, and Sydney looks at Lawrence as if expecting something important to follow, but nothing does.

A nurse arrives beside them with a tea trolley. 'Cup of tea, Lawrence?' he says.

'Yes, please,' says Lawrence.

The nurse is handing one over when he sees the cup of tea that Lawrence has on his lap. He rolls his eyes and offers the cup to Lewis instead. Lewis hesitates. He does want a cup of tea but there are alternatives on the trolley, at which he looks. They have camomile, *calming*. He does not want calming. There is a bottle of Edie's bubble bath at home in the bathroom, and that is lavender, *calming*, but he does not use it. He considers again the normal tea, but the nurse has already turned away and is offering it to Sydney, who asks for a cup of milk. The nurse is thrown by this request but provides the milk anyway. Lewis watches Sydney gulping it down. He thinks now that he would like milk too, but the nurse with the tea trolley has already moved on.

Sydney, wiping off his milk moustache, says to Lawrence, 'How was Billy Graham?'

Lawrence, who has picked up his coconut macaroon, puts it down again, a fond look coming over his face, his eyes lighting up, a shy smile lifting the corners of his mouth. 'Billy Graham?' he says, wearing an expression such as one might have when recalling a long-ago lover and finding oneself unexpectedly saying their name. 'Yes, we saw Billy Graham.'

'I saw him again,' says Lewis, 'the last time he came here, in 1989. I took Ruth.' He had been expecting Billy Graham in person, like the first time. Even as he entered the tent that had been erected in a field at the edge of the nearby town, he thought he was going to see the man himself. He was disappointed to realise that he was only going to see Billy Graham on a screen, that he was appearing by satellite, beamed from London. Someone fainted, though, nonetheless. People left their plastic chairs and walked down the aisle of sun-warmed grass, disappearing behind the screens as if, thought Lewis, they had gone to take a peek at the Wizard of Oz.

'That's right,' says Lawrence. 'I couldn't go because your mother had booked a cruise. I thought I'd get another chance to see him. She'd always wanted to go on a cruise. She said it would be a dream come true. Oh, it was dreadful.' He talks about the violent diarrhoea they and everyone else on board went down with—they suspected the salad. And then he talks about a British cruise ship recently turned away from Argentina. And he talks about the *Khian Sea* incident that was taking place the year before their cruise—the cargo ship carrying thousands of tons of nonhazardous waste, unable to dock. 'For more than two years they went from port to port, from country to country, unable to stop anywhere. Imagine being stuck on a ship, at sea and wanting to get home, all that time.'

'Yes,' says Lewis.

Sydney is watching him. 'You think you might like it,' he says.

Lewis does not say anything. He looks at the coconut macaroon that is going to waste in the saucer of his father's teacup.

'It was a ship carrying thousands of tons of ash,' says Sydney. 'It wasn't a cruise ship. It wasn't the Love Boat. You'd go stir crazy after a while.'

'Seeing Billy Graham,' says Lawrence, 'encouraged me to take action. I stopped reading D.H. Lawrence and after a while I gave up teaching literature altogether.' He is back, then, to expounding on the rot that had spoiled his D.H. Lawrence, his *Lady Chatterley's Lover*. It was no longer possible to enjoy the great tufts of primroses under the hazels, the dandelions making suns, the first daisies, the columbines and campions, and new-mown hay, and oak-tufts and honeysuckle. The novel seemed soiled. Creeping jenny would always now make him think of a penis—'a man's penis,' he says. And *Women in Love*, beginning with embroidery and yellow celandines, soon turned to the dangling yellow male catkin and the inseminatory yellow pollen and then came the descent into naked men wrestling and they 'penetrate into the very quick', they 'drive their white flesh deeper', they 'heave', 'working nearer and nearer', and just thinking about it now, Lawrence is reminded how he felt whenever Lewis was going off to or coming back from Sydney Flynn's house, or when he opened Lewis's bedroom door and saw them there on the bed together, and although he never actually caught them doing anything, everything was suggested. This was the novel that finally forced him to abandon his post at the school. He speaks about it through lips gone small and tight. The book, he says, is all about homosexuals and therefore he could not advocate it. He could not ask his students to study a book like that, a book with homoerotic undertones. He could not talk to them about one man feeling that way about another. He is getting agitated. He found that when he ceased to read D.H. Lawrence, he ceased to read literature at all, favouring theological works.

Lewis has not read *Lady Chatterley's Lover*; he has only read the dry account of its trial. He has read

Women in Love, in which two men wrestle naked on the carpet.

'But it's about more than that,' says Sydney. 'It's about a longing for a new world.'

Lawrence turns to Sydney and stares hard at him, narrowing his eyes again, frowning. 'I know who you are,' he says.

'Come on,' says Sydney to Lewis, 'let's go.' He stands, and as he does so his knee bangs against Lawrence's, upsetting the cup and saucer still balanced on the old man's bony thighs, spilling stone-cold tea into his lap. While Sydney walks away, heading into the entrance hall, passing the woman who cannot get home, making his way out into the parking lot, Lewis hurries off to find a cloth. When he comes back, his father says, 'Is Billy Graham still alive?'

Lewis, wiping down his father's trousers and his chair, says that he is.

'I want to go and see him,' says Lawrence.

'I don't know, Dad,' says Lewis. 'He's in his nineties. He doesn't tour any more. He's retired.'

'I want to see him.'

'We'll see.'

As he leaves, his father says, 'God loves you.'

When Lewis was little, his father always said at bedtime and on parting, 'Your mother loves you.' This was corroborated in junior school, where Lewis received the same message while eating his sandwiches in the dinner hall, until the day when he was instead told otherwise. Some years later, when Lewis began to live away from home, in halls of residence, his father took to saying, on doorsteps and train station platforms and over the telephone, 'God loves you,' and Lewis always felt that it was surely only a matter of time until someone suddenly said to him, 'God doesn't love you,' and that would be that.

When Lewis gets outside, he looks for the Saab and instead of seeing Sydney standing beside it he sees another man. Sydney is lying on the ground near the driver's door. The other man is standing above him, talking calmly down at him, with a boot on Sydney's groin. It takes a moment for Lewis to place him, to realise that this is Mrs Bolton's son.

Barry is saying, 'I want my money.'

'I haven't got it,' says Sydney.

Barry says again, more slowly, 'I want my money.'

Lewis does not hear what Sydney says, but he sees Barry's boot move and he hears Sydney yelling out.

'I'll take the car, then,' says Barry. The driver's door is standing wide open, and Barry gets in. The key must be in the ignition because he sets off so fast that it is the momentum that slams the door shut.

With the car gone and only the fumes lingering in the dusk, Lewis makes his way across the parking lot to the spot where Sydney is now getting to his feet, but Sydney is in turn setting off after the car, and the dog that is still in the back.

HE WANTS THE IMPOSSIBLE

THERE ARE FOUR mugs in the office. The two that are Ruth's say, 'TEA' and, 'COFFEE'. She does not drink coffee—the 'COFFEE' mug is her soup mug, although this bothers her a bit. Norman's number one mug says, 'WORLD'S BEST BOSS'. The other one says, 'I ♥ MY COMPUTER'.

Norman brings his favourite mug to his mouth, his lips reaching for the rim. The coffee—made from a big, cheap jar of brown dust that he is working his way through—is too hot. He sucks at the surface of it, at the coffee-scented steam, and then puts the mug down. 'So how was your morning off?' he says.

'All right, thank you,' says Ruth, without looking up from her work.

'So what's with the face?' When Ruth doesn't answer, Norman asks, 'What were you doing anyway?'

'Waiting in for a washing machine,' she says. The window is open and she can hear the children in the school playground, the blur of a few hundred shrieking voices. Standing up to close the window, she adds, 'It didn't come.'

'They never do,' says Norman. 'Have you rung them?'

'No,' says Ruth.

'Ring them. Tell them it was supposed to arrive this morning and you bloody well want it this morning.'

'But it's not this morning any more.'

'Ring them anyway.'

'I will.' She won't though, because there is no new washing machine. She invented the new washing machine because she did not want to have to say to Norman that she was going to meet a man, a stranger, an ex-con.

Sydney is not a total stranger—Ruth and he have exchanged many letters—but they have never met. She does not know what he looks like; she is not sure how old he is. He once mentioned that he liked the Rolling Stones.

And it is so much easier to say to Norman that her new washing machine was not delivered than that this man never showed.

'Are you wearing lipstick?' asks Norman. 'You don't usually wear lipstick.' When she does not answer, he adds, as he picks up his mug, ready to try the coffee again, 'The colour suits you.'

She wasn't late. She left her dad's house with more than enough time to spare. She did not take the direct route between the villages; she went a long way round, going through town, driving away from her destination before circling back. She drove past a car showroom, eyeing the shiny, family cars parked outside with large numbers in their windshields. She drove past the horse that lives at the edge of the industrial estate in a triangle of field too small for galloping in. She drove past the train station, from where trains go all the way to London St Pancras, and from there the Eurostar takes you under the sea to Paris, and then a fast train will take you to the south of France, or elsewhere. She always meant to take a trip on the Orient Express, to go from Paris to Istanbul, although apparently they stopped doing that route before she was born and the Orient Express no longer runs at all. There is a modern substitute, though. You can ride in the same old carriages along the same old routes and she thinks that would be wonderfully exciting.

Despite the detour, the killing of a surplus half hour, she still had a little bit of time in hand when she arrived at the strange little café that stood alone on a slope in Nether. Nervous in her new red coat, she pushed open the door and a bell rang over her head. These bells they have above the doors of cafés and sweet shops always make her feel like one of Pavlov's dogs.

Inside, there was only one customer, a woman with a baby held to her bare breast, a coffee cup on the table in front of her. Ruth watched the baby feeding, his fat hands clawing at his mother's breast, his fat legs kicking. When she caught the mother's eye, Ruth looked away.

At the counter, Ruth asked for decaffeinated tea and was told by the man (who was wearing a floral apron and a badge that said, 'How Can I Help You?') that there was none. She accepted normal tea instead ('but not too strong') and took it to a table near the woman. She observed the woman drinking her coffee whilst feeding her baby and said to her, 'Is that decaffeinated?'

The woman looked up. 'No,' she said.

'You shouldn't have caffeine when you're breastfeeding,' said Ruth. 'Stimulants are bad for the baby. He won't be able to sleep.'

The mother, ignoring her, finished off her coffee and ordered a refill.

After a while, Ruth went back to the counter to ask the man for another cup of tea. The mother left with her baby, and Ruth sat there alone, glancing up at the door from time to time, even though it did not open and the bell did not ring. After two cups of tea and a bowl of soup, she paid and went back out onto the street. Over the road, on a well-tended green, a man was sitting on a bench—he had been there throughout, she thought. He was smoking a cigarette, or so she supposed, but when she crossed the road to speak to him, to ask if he was Sydney, she discovered that the white stick he kept putting to and taking from between his lips was not a cigarette but the stick of a lollipop. She stood in front of him and he crunched what was left.

'Excuse me,' she said to this man, who was perhaps in his fifties, 'are you Sydney?'

He looked at her with interest. 'Who's asking?' he said.

Something about the look of him, the glint in his eye, made her walk away, regardless of whether or not he was Sydney. She got into her car, put her Susan Boyle CD back to track two and drove away.

'I've got a meeting,' says Norman, getting up from behind his desk. He puts on his jacket and is walking away when, turning his head, he says, 'Those flyers need to go out this afternoon.'

'They won't be ready till Friday,' says Ruth.

'They need to go out this afternoon,' he says again, leaving the room.

Ruth, glancing at the clock, picks up the phone and calls the printers. She lets it ring for a while but there is no answer and she hangs up. She leans down to look inside the bag she has under her desk. As well as the Tupperware tub that she picked up from her dad's house this morning, there is an apple that needs eating. She will wash the tub at home this evening before refilling it with the soup she will make for dinner. She thinks she must smell of soup, of vegetables, of waning fruit, most of the time. She looks at the clock again but only minutes have passed and home time is still a long way off.

She doesn't really know why she started corresponding with Sydney. She wasn't looking for a relationship, although she was single, not yet married to John—this was years ago. She wouldn't have said she was lonely; she was busy at work. Amongst her responsibilities was the administration of the writing competition into which Sydney had entered a very long love poem. She noticed from the address on his entry form that he was in prison. A couple of months later, she had to write to say that he had been unsuccessful, and he had written back to say that she seemed like a beautiful person. She put his letter into the recycling bin before taking it out again. She kept it in her 'pending' tray for three weeks before replying to him.

When he sent another letter, she recognised the stationery and his handwriting straight away. Norman was at his desk, looking at her without seeing her while he talked on the phone. Using a pair of scissors as a letter opener (thinking of her granddad and the real and rather fine letter opener that lived on a small table inches from his letterbox in the house on Small Street) she sliced open the envelope. 'What have you got there?' said Norman, whose phone call had finished and who was watching her, and she wondered if it was just the care she had taken with the envelope that made him ask, or perhaps she had been smiling. 'Just junk,' she said, and when he wasn't looking she stole it into the soup bag at her feet.

Sydney told her, in the letters he sent, that he had grown up not far at all from where she was; that he had gone to school in the village in which she worked (*the village in which you work—and live?*, he wrote). He worked, he said, in the prison library and spent a lot of time reading, and writing; he was a published writer, he said, and Ruth imagined a poem published in a village newsletter, as one of hers had once been. He said that when he got out, when he was a free man, he wanted to travel all over the world. She is not sure he'll be able to, with a criminal record. She expects that many countries will turn him away.

When, some months later, she began a relationship with John, she stopped writing to Sydney, and eventually heard nothing from him until he wrote to say that he was coming out of prison (*the first thing I'll do is go and get my dog*) and would like to meet up. By then, Ruth was married, and she'd had a son. (Full of pethidine, she'd been split in two without feeling the pain.) At first, she thought she wouldn't go, that she wouldn't meet him, but this morning she set off in her car, in a new red coat, and she knew that she would go to the café after all.

She picks up the phone again, dials the printers and listens to the ringing for a while before replacing the receiver.

Sydney picked the venue, suggested the date and time. She wonders why he changed his mind. That might have been him sitting on the bench, getting a good look at her first. She feels rather foolish.

She is eating her apple when she suddenly thinks, 'It was a scam. He was just getting me out of the house so that he could burgle me.' And then she thinks, 'But he wasn't getting me out of the house, he was getting me out of work. He doesn't know where I live.' Frowning, she finishes the apple. There were girls at school who would eat the whole thing, the core, the pips, the calyx. She found it astonishing. She throws her core away.

Norman, returning from his meeting, settling himself at his desk, says, 'Did your friend show up?'

'What?' says Ruth, looking up quickly.

'A friend of yours was here, asking for you. I thought it was your dad at first, because of his age. Is he a family friend?'

'What was his name?'

'Stanley or Sidney, something like that. I told him you were at home waiting in for something. I asked if he knew where you lived and he said he did. He didn't come and see you?'

'No,' says Ruth. She wonders why he said he knew where she lived. Just so as not to appear suspicious, she supposes, having come to the office pretending to be a friend, when in fact, no doubt, he was hoping to burgle it in her absence. Presumably, he was in ca-hoots with the man on the bench whose job it was to let Sydney know that she was safely installed in the café.

'Where are we with the print? Is it ready?'

'There's no one there,' says Ruth. 'No one's picking up the phone.'

'They must be there,' says Norman. 'I want that print today. If they're not picking up, you'd better go there in person.'

Ruth puts on her coat ('New coat?' asks Norman) and picks up her handbag. As she heads through the door, Norman calls out to her, 'Are you going anywhere near a bakery?'

'No,' says Ruth.

She steps outside, into the cold, fresh air, and as her feet hit the pavement she recalls an evening the previous week when she got the feeling that she was being followed home from work, although, whenever she turned to look behind her, she could see no one there, and nothing happened.

She gets into her car, and into her mind comes the possibility that it was Sydney that evening, following her home so that he would know where she lived and could break in while she was wasting her time in that strange little café. Except that she was not going home; she was on her way to her dad's to look at his computer. He'd been getting emails he didn't want. 'They're still sending those emails,' he said, as if they were like nuisance calls, somebody hounding him. She does not usually visit him in the evening, but she had not been surprised to find him right where she had left him that morning, in his armchair. She thought at first that he was praying, the way his head was bowed towards the lamplight, but he was asleep.

She turns around, no longer heading for town, heading instead towards her dad's house, worrying about the possibility of a break-in, and the likelihood—Ruth, in her little car, speeds up—that her dad would have been at home at the time, the burglar giving him a surprise.

HE WANTS TO
SEE TWO MEN
WRESTLING NAKED
ON THE CARPET

LEWIS STANDS FOR a minute outside the nursing home, in the darkening parking lot. He considers going back inside, braving the woman who grabs at his wrist as he goes by, but instead he walks home.

He goes slowly, resting often, leaning on a lamppost, a bin, a low wall, pushing his tongue against a shard of walnut stuck in his tooth. He wonders if Sydney will come back.

He feels his cell phone—the one Ruth gave to him for emergencies—trembling against his thigh. He puts his hand into his trouser pocket and realises that the phone is still in the kitchen drawer, no doubt with the battery run down. The trembling he felt against his leg was a phantom; it was his body playing tricks on him.

The tune the phone plays when someone is trying to get in touch with him is something Ruth put on there, or else it came with the phone. It is the same tune they play in the doctor's waiting room and down the phone when they have you on hold and when the ice cream van is coming. It is as if it is the only song there is, the only piece of music in the world.

When Lewis opens his front door and finds someone standing in his hallway, it takes him a moment to adjust to the fact that it is not Sydney but Ruth.

'Where the hell have you been?' she says, and her cursing, her saying 'hell' like that, makes him flinch. Lewis has never spoken that way. He thinks of Sydney saying *Jesus fucking Christ*. What if he were to talk like that? He imagines saying to her now, *Jesus fucking Christ, Ruth. Chill out.* That's how they talk, the young people: *Chill out. Take a chill pill.*

'I thought something had happened to you,' says Ruth.

Lewis has to wait for her to take a few steps back before he can get inside and close the door behind him. 'Nothing's happened,' he says.

'You've had your hair cut,' she says. 'And you've done something else as well.' She studies his face while Lewis looks over her shoulder into his house. 'Where are your glasses?'

'They got broken,' says Lewis, moving past her towards the stairs, where he sits down to take off his shoes.

Ruth stands over him. 'I've been on the phone to everyone,' she says.

'I went to see Granddad,' says Lewis. 'Why are you here?'

'I was worried about you. I tried ringing your cell but I couldn't get you. Your phone's in the kitchen drawer.'

Pulling on his slippers, Lewis stands again and hangs up his coat. 'What were you ringing for?' he asks, as he limps down the hallway towards the living room.

'Have you walked all the way from the home? For God's sake, Dad.' She goes with him and gets him settled into his chair. 'Where's your spare pair of glasses?' she asks.

'I don't know,' says Lewis.

Ruth looks in the kitchen but doesn't find them, just the empty case in the drawer. Coming out again, she says, 'Why have you got sake? Have you been into town? Have you been to the new deli?'

'No. Do they sell it there?'

'You won't like it. You only like shandy.'

Before she leaves, she makes Lewis a cup of milky tea, and as she hands it to him, he says, 'Have you ever had Goldschläger?'

'*Goldschläger?*' she says. 'What's got into you? Yes,' she adds, going into the hallway to get her coat, 'I have.' She comes back into the living room with his broken glasses in her hand. 'I'll take these for mending,' she says, leaning over him and kissing him near the corner of his eye.

When Ruth has gone, Lewis goes into the kitchen. Edie's best pie dish is still on the floor. The sake is still on the table. Ruth was right—he does not like anything strong. He is not like John used to be, passionately opposed to alcohol and pouring away gifts of wine; Lewis just does not much like the taste.

He opens the sake and puts the carton to his nose. He does not like the smell. He takes a glass down from the cupboard and pours out a measure. He looks at it, this exotic drink from the golden carton. He lifts the glass to his lips and takes a sip. It makes him grimace; it is like drinking vinegar. He tries to bring it close to his mouth again but he can't bring himself to do it. He wants to like it, but he does not.

He puts the glass down by the sink. He ought to give the sake to Ruth but he isn't sure that he will. He screws the top back onto the carton and puts it away in the fridge.

The soup is there, on the middle shelf. He takes it out and cuts some brown bread to eat with it, as much brown bread as he can swallow, so much brown bread that when he finally stands up, his belly is hard.

He goes upstairs, tonguing that shard of walnut still stuck in his teeth. It has survived the milky tea, the soup and brown bread, and might even survive the brushing of his teeth, the Sensodyne.

It is early but he gets undressed and puts on his pyjamas, leaving his underwear on underneath and wearing his dressing gown on top because he is cold. He slides his feet into his slippers and ties the belt of his dressing gown, feeling something hard in the pocket. Dipping his hand in, he retrieves his spare glasses. When he puts them on, he sees his world again, everything just as it was.

He goes through to Ruth's bedroom, switches on his computer and checks his emails. 'Joy,' says one, giving him a price for Viagra. 'Live the life you've always wanted to lead,' says another, which might be selling watches although it is unclear. The one under that says, 'Make your Asian dreams come true,' and Lewis thinks of Sydney gazing through the window of the travel agency. 'We miss you,' says an email from a furniture company that Lewis has never used. 'Get it while you can!' He clicks 'Get Mail' again but there is nothing in the ether waiting to come through.

Leaving the computer, he goes to the foot of the stairs to fetch the little book of nursery rhymes out of his coat pocket, but when he looks at it with his glasses on he sees that it is not the book of nursery rhymes after all; it is some other book of similar size and appearance. Instead of taking it up to bed, he finds a space for it on the bookshelves, alongside his father's spurned Lawrences, his *Lady Chatterley's Lover* and the coverage of its trial, and *The Rainbow*, all copies of which were at one time seized and burnt, the book banned, and not that long ago, he thinks; less than a lifetime ago. He ought to have *Women in Love* somewhere as well but he doesn't know where that's got to. Lewis has never seen the film. He wants to. He meant to look for it in HMV.

A few of the books, he sees, are out of order. *Another Time, Another Place, Another Man*, which ought to be in with his father's theology books, has instead been put on Edie's shelf, while one of Edie's, with 'Rapture' in the title, is next to his father's Bibles. He puts the theology book back in its place and takes down the Bliss Tempest, on whose cover there is a naked male torso, brown and hard and gleaming like the furniture in the nursing home after it's been buffed with Mr Sheen. Lewis, who has never shown much interest in Edie's books, takes another one off the shelf. Reading what is written on the back, he wonders for the first time whether this is the romance he's always assumed it to be, whether this is not in fact erotica, pornography. The font on the cracked spines and on the covers is like handwriting, as if these were not books but very long letters.

Removing his glasses again, he goes upstairs and into his bedroom. He will say a prayer and climb into bed. He will lie on his side, either turned towards Edie's half of the bed or turned away, or he will lie on his back, looking up at the ceiling, thinking about the boy who is afraid of the dark, afraid when he wakes in the middle of the night, wanting something. It is not easy to get comfortable these days. It is always in bed at night that he feels new twinges in his teeth. It is when he is lying there in the dark that he finds himself thinking about people fainting for Billy Graham, about what it would be like to be immersed by the Reverend, about frozen embryos that, removed from the freezer, pop. It is when he closes his eyes that he thinks about the night of the school reunion, when he walked away from the school hall, the spinning disco ball and 'The Final Countdown', coming to a stop at the far end of the corridor, outside the chemistry laboratory. As he stood there, recalling the screaming jelly baby experiment that his colleague had performed, the astonishing flare, he tried the door and found it unlocked.

Closing the door behind him, he went to the front of the classroom and stood behind the long bench on which the teacher's demonstrations took place. Behind him were the cupboards in which the equipment was stored. He opened the cupboard doors. He knew where everything was kept. He knew how to put it together.

He had it all set up when the door opened. 'This is where I do chemistry, Gran,' said a boy, walking in, followed by a woman with dyed-red hair and a dog-tooth coat over her arm.

Seeing Lewis, she said to him, 'Ah! Are you going to do a demonstration for us?'

Lewis, smiling, put his hand in his pocket and brought out a bag of jelly babies. 'I am indeed,' he said. The woman and the boy sat down on the pupils' stools, the woman behind the desk and the boy in front. Lewis waited until they were settled and then he said, 'Watch this.' He lit his Bunsen burner, heated the chemical compound in a beaker and dropped in a handful of jelly babies. What followed was so bright that Lewis did not see at first that the boy was holding his face, that he had his hands to his eyes; it took him a moment to realise that the howling was coming not from the jelly babies but from the boy's grandmother.

He does not yet know if the boy will see again. John brings occasional news from The Golden Fleece, which is run by the boy's father.

Looking out of his bedroom window before closing the curtains, Lewis finds himself staring at a car that is parked a little way up the road. It is outside the men's toilet, whose light is on. The darkness and the streetlights make it hard to tell the colour of the car, but he thinks it is a Saab, and he can see a shape that might be a dog on the back seat. He can't see anyone else, a driver.

He goes back downstairs. He does not stop to put on his shoes but goes outside in his slippers, pulling the door to behind him. He can feel, through his slippers' thin soles, the cold, hard ground. He is aware of the inadequacy of his dressing gown against the night's chill, compared to his warm winter coat. He is missing the familiar warmth of his hair against his neck. His sideburns are keeping his cheeks warm though, and he at least has his underwear on.

Lewis walks—his bad knee aching—up his side of the street. Crossing over the road, he approaches the car. He is sure, now, as he draws closer, that it is Sydney's car, Sydney's dog. She is watching him and looks happy to see him. If the car is unlocked, he will fetch her out.

Lewis tries the driver's door, and it opens. He takes a look at the ignition but the key is not there. He is reaching for the dog when he pauses, looking at her, looking at the brandy barrel around her neck. Instead of leading her out, he gets hold of the brandy barrel, opens it up and finds the spare key inside.

As quietly as he can, he gets into the driver's seat and closes the door. He is aware of the deterioration in his eyesight since he last sat behind a steering wheel. He slips his hand into his dressing gown pocket for his spare pair of glasses, but he has lost them again. He will have to drive slowly.

Starting the car, he pulls away from the curb. He had assumed that a left-hand drive would feel stranger than it does. The Saab might be old but it handles nicely.

He has barely gone any distance when he sees that the front door of his house is standing wide open. Pulling up outside his gate, he gets out, going as quickly as he can up the garden path, with a shooting pain in his knee. He closes the door properly, slamming it. It strikes him that he does not have his door key but there isn't time to think about that now. The back door is probably still unlocked. He ought not to dash off in that case, knowing that the house might not be secure, but he has to get going. He has turned around and is coming back down his path when he sees Barry Bolton standing outside the toilets, looking down the road at him. 'You!' he shouts. 'Sullivan!' Lewis gets himself back to the car, climbs in behind the wheel and drives off again, going faster than Barry can run, his adrenalin soaring as he tops twenty miles per hour in the Saab.

His first thought is to turn around and drive up to the nursing home; to take the dog inside to show to his father, who would like to see a golden retriever. But then he realises that Barry might follow him there, and it also occurs to him that visiting hours are over so he would not be allowed in anyway. His father will be in bed; they will all be in bed or on their way. He cannot linger around here though. Instead, he drives out of the village towards the only place he thinks he might find Sydney.

HE WANTS A
TIME MACHINE

THE DRIVE IS excruciating. In constant anticipation of someone or something unseen in the darkness running into the road, with his foot ready to jump on the brake and his knee throbbing, Lewis heads out of the village. There is someone on the pavement near the mailbox, and someone else strolling alone with an empty dog lead, but when Lewis slows down beside them, he sees that they are not Sydney, and he drives on again.

He gets onto the main road, which will take him from one village to another, or into town if he were to take a different turning. He considers doing it, driving into town, something he has not done for years. He could buy a new coat; he could buy a new suit, or something more fashionable, for going out in. He could find Sydney and take him to the movies.

There is a cinema in town that shows 3D films. If you wear the correct glasses, the images come right out of the screen towards you and it seems as if you could touch them or that they might touch you. He has never seen one of these films. Ruth's boy has seen one. There were birds, said the boy, that flew out of the screen, and shooting stars that fell towards you, and it was like you could reach out and catch them. 'And could you?' said Lewis. 'Could you catch them?' 'Well, no,' said the boy, 'you couldn't *actually* catch them,' and he looked at his granddad as if he were a fool for thinking it. 'And there were bubbles,' said the boy, 'that popped right in front of your face.'

Another day, Lewis tells himself; he'll do all that another day, when he has not come out wearing his pyjamas and slippers, when he has not come out without his glasses and his wallet. Anyone finding him wandering around town like this would only want to send him back to whatever institution he'd come from.

There is a man walking along the verge, wading through the long grass in between the road and the hedge. Lewis slows down beside him and when the man turns towards him, Lewis sees the yellow top beneath the open coat.

Sydney, seeing the Saab and expecting Barry Bolton, runs, hopping awkwardly between the uneven verge and the gutter. Lewis has to drive along beside him with the window down, saying, 'It's me, Sydney, it's Lewis,' so that Sydney will stop running.

'What are you doing in my car?' says Sydney. He is leaning over with one hand on his knee, out of breath, and one hand on his heart. 'How did you get the car?'

'I saw it parked outside the public toilet,' says Lewis, 'while Barry Bolton was using the facilities. I took it.'

'Where are you going?'

'I was looking for you,' says Lewis. 'I figured you might be staying at your parents' house.'

'You figured right,' says Sydney.

Lewis moves into the passenger seat so that Sydney can get in behind the wheel. Sydney greets his dog, and at the same time pushes her eager face away from him. They drive on, and Sydney tells Lewis all about Barry Bolton, who lives in Nether, the village towards which they are now heading.

'Does he know where you live?' asks Lewis.

'Yes,' says Sydney.

'He knows where I live too.'

They drive through the countryside in darkness, the kind of darkness that is not found in cities but is found in the countryside, in between villages. When they pass a sign that says, 'Concealed entrance', Sydney, slowing just enough, takes the turning. The dog, staggering, starts to whine.

'Do you remember,' says Sydney, 'the last time you were in this car? I picked you up from Small Street.'

'It was my first time as well as my last,' says Lewis. It was early in the summer of 1961, the day Sydney brought round the puppy, Old Yeller. They drove around for a while and then Sydney took Lewis to his parents' house in Nether, where they sat talking in Sydney's bedroom. Lewis remembers looking at Sydney's teeth while he was speaking, at the spike of his canines and the sharp incisors that he had once seen biting into another boy's ear, Sydney bearing down on the boy like Dracula. Sitting on the edge of Sydney's bed, looking at Sydney's teeth and thinking about Sydney fighting in the playground, Lewis said, 'Have you ever tried jiu-jitsu?' He had to look away before adding, 'I'll show you what I can, if you like.' At that moment, though, Sydney's mother had come in with a plate of home-made biscuits and when she had gone neither of them mentioned the jiu-jitsu again. They ate some of the cookies and then Lewis said, 'Perhaps I should be going.'

'Don't go yet,' said Sydney. For a little while, neither spoke. They finished the cookies and then Sydney said, 'So what do you want to do?'

'What?' said Lewis.

'What do you want to do with your life?'

'Oh,' said Lewis. 'I don't really know. What about you?'

'I want to be a writer,' said Sydney. 'I'll read you a story I've written.' He reached over to his desk and pulled a few paper-clipped pages from a sheaf bound by an elastic band. Lewis remembers thinking that if he had written a story, he would not have left it lying out on his desk like that, where anyone might pick it up and read it; he would have put it away in a drawer or hidden it under his mattress.

He sat and watched while Sydney read from the handwritten pages, and when he stopped reading, Lewis said, 'Is that it? Have you not written the ending yet?'

'That is the ending,' said Sydney.

'Oh,' said Lewis. 'So the guy doesn't get what he wants?'

'No,' said Sydney. 'He doesn't get what he wants. You didn't like it?'

Lewis shrugged. He wanted there to be another page. 'I thought he would get what he wanted in the end.'

'Oh,' said Sydney. 'No.'

Sydney sat looking at the pages in his hands, and Lewis, recalling the moment, is reminded also of the look on Ruth's boy's face when the yellow-bellied newt he'd been aiming to catch was inadvertently crushed under Lewis's foot.

Now, as he drives down the narrow country lane, Sydney says, 'I didn't half get a bollocking from my old man when he realised I'd been driving his car.'

'It's lasted well,' says Lewis.

'I've been reading a book about the physics of the future,' says Sydney. 'In the future, we'll have driverless cars. Didn't you used to think we'd all have hovercars by now? Didn't you think we'd have time machines by the twenty-first century?'

Lewis—being driven down an unmarked lane lined with overgrown hedges, with trees arching above them so that it is like speeding through a tunnel, the road lit only by their own headlights, with Sydney's fist, on the gear stick, changing gear, bumping against his thigh—thinks that he would like a time machine.

'By the end of the century,' continues Sydney, 'there'll be astronauts on Mars.'

'I keep hearing about pills,' says Lewis, 'that can reverse the ageing process.'

'We'll be able to video our dreams.'

Lewis is not so sure he would want that. He is quiet for a moment and then Sydney interrupts the silence, saying, 'How many senses have you got?'

Lewis, suspecting that he is being tricked, says, anyway, 'Five.'

'You've got more than twenty,' says Sydney. 'You know when you've got an itch, and you have a sense of time, and pain, and hunger . . .'

Lewis looks at him, astonished to find that he has gone through life thinking that he only had five, the basic five senses, when all along he had more than twenty. Aware now of his embarrassment of senses, Lewis pictures himself like the sensory homunculus, a man with grossly enlarged lips and tongue and genitals, and the most enormous hands. Thinking about whether he's got an itch makes him feel that he has.

At the end of the lane, they come to what was once countryside but is now all built up, housing estates extending over what used to be fields. Lewis is on the point of saying to Sydney, 'Do you remember when this was all fields?' but he doesn't want to sound like an old man, he doesn't want to sound like his own father, so he doesn't say anything.

And then, coasting down the final hill, the figure on the dashboard performing a wild hula on the rough track, they emerge into Nether, into the village square. Sydney starts to slow down. They approach the café and Lewis peers towards it. Despite all that bread he ate, all that fibre, he thinks he might be peckish. He has never been into that café, whose door, the frame, is the yellow of a sunny-side-up egg, the same shade as a sign he's seen, strapped to a lamppost on the main road, that says, 'Better late than never'. He thinks about all the things they might sell in there, imagining all sorts of goodies he has never had: cappuccinos, espressos, carrot cake. Sydney is not stopping at the café though, and, besides, it looks as if it is on the point of closing.

They skirt the green, the bench standing empty in the middle, and Lewis looks at the blossom on the winter-flowering trees and, on the other side of the road, the rows of little stone cottages with neat, square gardens and window boxes. It is a nice village, he thinks; it would be a pleasant place to live, were it not for Barry Bolton.

Sydney pulls up outside the house that is still bare-bricked between its clad neighbours. Lewis half-expects to see Sydney's father in the front garden or at the front window, shooing him away.

'There's no one here,' says Sydney, and Lewis is not sure whether he means his parents or Barry Bolton.

They get out and let the dog out too.

There are all sorts of parking restrictions in town and even in Lewis's village now—spots that you are not allowed to park in, entire streets that are for permit holders only. He does not know about here. Lewis has never parked somewhere he shouldn't; he has never had a parking ticket tucked under his windshield wiper. He has never had a speeding ticket or been stopped by the police and given a verbal warning. When he was at school, other boys were given warnings and final warnings by police officers and park keepers, but such things never happened to Lewis. He did get that letter though, recently, about spending too long in the parking lot of the supermarket on Small Street. He would like to go back to the playground, to say to the boys, when they boast about the trouble they've been in, that he has had a letter threatening him with court. He ought to have kept the letter as proof that he parked for much longer than was allowed.

In truth, though, he was mortified to receive that letter. The experience was quite unpleasant and he hopes that he has heard the last of it. He paid the fine promptly. The moment the letter came through the door, he wrote a cheque, put a first-class stamp on the envelope and took it straight down to the postbox. He put the threatening letter, with its assertion of video evidence and the scales of justice in the corner, into the recycling, feeling the sweat in his armpits, on his clean shirt. He made a cup of tea to help himself calm down.

'Cup of tea?' says Sydney, as if, thinks Lewis, briefly alarmed, Sydney can see right into his head, as if he can see what Lewis thinks about.

'Not for me, thank you,' he says—he does not normally have caffeine this late, so close to bedtime—but Sydney is already walking away with the dog at his heels. Lewis cuts across the front garden. Seeing his own slippered feet nipping across the lawn, he feels like an escapee, like one of the residents getting out of the nursing home in the middle of the night. He follows Sydney down the side of the house and in through the kitchen door.

HE DOES NOT
WANT THE BOY
TO BE SPOILED

EVEN WITHOUT HIS glasses on, Lewis can see that the units in Sydney's kitchen are the originals. The fixtures and fittings, the table and chairs and the lino floor tiles must be as old as he is. He wants to say to Edie, 'Look, this kitchen is older than ours and is just fine.' But it is years since Edie won that argument, years since they had their new units put in, their new floor laid.

'What do you want?' asks Sydney, opening cupboards, offering cocoa, Horlicks, Ribena, but Lewis says no, no—he does not want any of these things.

Sydney, with hands still dirty from lying on the ground being kicked by Barry Bolton, fills the kettle and opens a cupboard. Looking for teabags, he finds Marmite that is years past its best before date and a jar of pickled beetroot gone brown and soft and falling apart. 'I didn't think these things ever went off,' he says, opening the pedal bin to dispose of these expired products and finding it stuffed full. 'Empty the bin,' says Sydney. If Sydney were Ruth's boy, Lewis would say, '*Please. Please* empty the bin.' When he does this, he sounds as if he is begging, pleading with him. '*Please*,' he says as he stands there holding the last cookie just out of the boy's reach, 'I want it, *please*.'

Lewis reaches down, knots the top of the garbage bag and lifts it out. Taking the rubbish to the back door, he steps outside and makes his way to the garbage bin. It is, in that moment, as if he lives here, as if he lives here with Sydney, like the Odd Couple: Lewis puts the rubbish out while Sydney makes the tea.

His daydream is interrupted by the sound of breaking glass. It came from the street. He can't tell how close it was. He can hear children laughing and running.

Lewis lifts the lid of the garbage bin, to put the rubbish safely inside, but he finds the bin full to the brim. He has to leave the lid gaping, the bin bag exposed, balanced; it will be got at by foxes, which will tear it open.

He returns to the kitchen, where Sydney, having found what he needs, is making the tea, making a cup for Lewis as well. Sydney adds three sugars to his, and Lewis thinks of Ruth's boy, who asks for sugar sandwiches and leaves the licked bread on his plate, who wants jelly for breakfast and sweets while his mother is cooking the dinner and pink syrup in his bedtime milk. Lewis imagines the cavities that might already be forming in the boy's baby teeth.

The boy starts sentences with, 'I want,' before knowing what it is he really wants. 'I want,' he says, 'I want, I want, I want . . .' Even at night, in his sleep, the boy calls out, 'I want it!' and, 'Give it to me!'

Lewis does not want the boy to be spoiled.

They drink their tea sitting on the doorstep, eyeing the night. The children seem to have disappeared and it is quiet now. Sydney takes out his electronic cigarette and Lewis asks after his parents. 'My mum's long gone,' says Sydney. 'My dad died recently, after a fall.'

'Were you there?' asks Lewis.

Sydney shakes his head. Finishing his tea, he gets to his feet and goes inside. Lewis follows him.

'Come through,' says Sydney, treading on the heels of his trainers to take them off. He'll ruin them, thinks Lewis, watching him. Lewis leaves his slippers on because his feet are cold.

In the living room, Lewis looks around, taking in a faded version of familiar wallpaper dotted with pastoral scenes. Sydney, standing in front of a bookcase, removes one of the books. 'You left this here,' he says. Without his glasses on, Lewis can't read the title of the book, but he does not say so. Thanking Sydney, he takes it, putting it down on the coffee table.

'The house has been sold,' says Sydney. 'I'm going to go abroad.'

'Again?' says Lewis.

Sydney says nothing for a moment and then he says, 'I've never really seen another country.'

'What do you mean?' says Lewis. 'You were born in India.'

'I was little when we left. I don't remember it at all.'

'Oh,' says Lewis, recalling how Sydney, with his pins in his map, used to talk about going back there. 'Did you never go?' he says. 'You never visited the gold mines?'

'No,' says Sydney, going to a window and peering out. 'I don't think there's much left of them now. They were used as nuclear testing sites in the 1980s.' He draws the curtains.

'You've been to other countries though. You spent your whole childhood on army bases.'

'In England.'

'Oh,' says Lewis. 'But you've travelled. You've been to Tokyo and Thailand. You've been to Germany and Scandinavia.'

Sydney shakes his head. 'I've had a lot of time to read,' he says.

Lewis stares at Sydney, with the same look on his face that Lawrence had when he discovered that Lewis was not on the Sunday school trip that he ought to have been on and was instead up a tree behind the house. Looking out of an upstairs window, it had become clear to Lawrence that Lewis had not got on the bus to the seaside after all but had been on a branch all day long, reading books. Lewis remembers his father standing at the foot of the tree, calling up to him, 'You've got to come down sometime.' When Lewis finally descended, his father said to him, 'You live in books,' and then he took the books out of Lewis's hands and hid them somewhere.

Sydney goes around the room, drawing the rest of the curtains and putting on lamps.

'You wanted to see the Wonders of the World,' says Lewis.

'I haven't even seen one.'

'I think there's only one left, apart from ruins.'

'That's the old ones,' says Sydney. 'They add new ones all the time. I plan to see them all.'

He moves towards Lewis, raising his hand towards Lewis's cheek. 'What are these?' he says, tugging at Lewis's sideburns as if they might come off. 'Come upstairs,' he says. 'I'm going to take my clippers to these.'

Lewis reaches up and feels his own sideburns. 'I don't know,' he says, but even as he says this he is following Sydney into the hallway and up the stairs. They go past the open door of Sydney's bedroom and into the bathroom, where Sydney sits Lewis down on the toilet seat lid. He opens the bathroom cabinet and takes out some clippers, which he plugs into a 'SHAVERS ONLY' socket. Lewis wonders about this, about why such sockets should be for shavers only, and what would happen if he tried to plug in some other electrical item, something he shouldn't. The worst that could happen is that the appliance would not work, or the fuse might blow. He pictures electricity fizzing dangerously inside the ancient cables in the walls.

Sydney comes over to Lewis again, standing close to press the vibrating device against his skin, his jaw. Neither speaks. Lewis listens to the clippers' buzz, the sound both soft and loud like a lawnmower, like insects on a windowsill. The wiry hairs succumb with a crackling sound like static. Sydney moves around him, touching the head of the clippers to Lewis's cheekbones, brushing at Lewis's face with his free hand.

It does not take long. After no time at all, Sydney switches the clippers off, steps away and says, 'You're all done.'

Lewis stands and looks around for a mirror, but there isn't one.

'There's a mirror in my bedroom,' says Sydney, and he leads the way, although Lewis knows where it is, and he follows even though he won't be able to see himself clearly anyway.

He stands in front of the bedroom mirror, into whose frame Sydney has stuck postcards from around the world, pictures of places he wanted—or still wants—to visit. In the remaining space, Lewis can see his face in soft focus. He sits down on the edge of the bed, where he sat before, when the horses' hooves were drumming on the road outside and an ice cream van played 'Greensleeves', stopping halfway through, leaving a high note hanging in the air. Sydney sat next to him, his nearest leg pulled up onto the bed, his trousered knee pointing at Lewis, who suggested jiujitsu before being interrupted.

'Whose ear did you bite?' says Lewis.

'What?' says Sydney, frowning at him.

'You bit a boy's ear in the playground—whose was it?'

'Did I?' says Sydney. 'I don't remember.'

'You made me think of Dracula.'

Sydney shows his weathered teeth as he sits down next to Lewis. 'Tonight is mine,' says Sydney, and Lewis wonders what time it is. He looks around the room for a clock, not seeing one on the wall or on Sydney's bedside table or on his desk. He remembers Sydney's sheaf of stories, held together by a rubber band. He remembers someone—a scientist—talking about rubber bands that spend their life stretched around a package, the molecules in them pulled out straight, and the whole time they're straining to contract, trying desperately, year after year, to kink.

He says to Sydney, 'Do you still write?'

'Yes,' says Sydney, 'I still write.'

'Have you had anything published?'

'You're familiar with Bliss Tempest.'

'Yes,' says Lewis.

'I'm Bliss Tempest,' says Sydney.

It takes Lewis a moment to make sense of this. 'You're Bliss Tempest? You write the Bliss Tempest books? My wife read every single one.'

'Now I write stories in which everyone gets what they want,' says Sydney.

Lewis thinks about Edie's Bliss Tempest novels, the characters that Edie likened to him, the men to whom Sydney has given all kinds of adventures. He feels a touch of envy towards them.

Sydney reaches out and touches the back of Lewis's neck. The palm of his hand is rough. Lewis worries about the dirt on Sydney's fingers touching the neatly sewn-up wound near his hairline. He does not say anything though; he does not ask Sydney to take his hand away. Sydney gives the back of his neck a squeeze.

Lewis has just opened his mouth to say something else—'Oh,' he says—when Sydney reaches for the elasticated waist of Lewis's pyjama trousers. He leans in and Lewis feels Sydney's teeth on the soft lobe of his ear, and then his own fingers are touching Sydney's torso, feeling his ribs and the chest hairs that will be grey or white beneath the yellow T-shirt whose logo means 'Just Do It'; he is dressed like a boy. And Lewis, too, wearing pyjamas with a vest underneath, feels like a boy on a sleepover, or an old-age pensioner.

He has some trouble with the button on Sydney's trousers, due to a touch of stiffness in his joints; it is worse in the winter. Then the button falls off and

Lewis picks it up off the bedding and puts it some-where safe—on the bedside table—for sewing on again later.

He turns back to Sydney, who is lying down now, with his grey hair against the primrose yellow of his pillowcase. Lewis lies down next to him. Comfortable between Sydney and the wall, he could almost close his eyes and sleep.

He does not though. Instead, they make so much noise that the dog, downstairs somewhere, starts barking, and she is still barking when they are lying, later, exhausted on the floor, each feeling the weight of the other—an arm across a chest, a thigh across a thigh—and Sydney with his hand on his own heart.

HE WANTS TO
ALWAYS BE HERE

LEWIS IS SLOWER than Sydney to get dressed again, slower to get himself up off the floor and leave the bedroom. By the time he gets down to the living room, Sydney is standing smoking his electronic cigarette, scowling at it. Lewis moves towards the sofa, not quite sure what to say.

'Don't forget your book,' says Sydney.

Lewis, who has reached the coffee table, comes to a stop and picks up his book. He looks at the cover, as a browser in a bookshop might, although it is all just a blur. He looks as if he is about to say something, perhaps about the book, or about the last time he was here.

'Come on, then,' says Sydney. 'I'll drive you home.'

They go into the kitchen where Sydney puts on his coat and shoes and picks up his rucksack. Lewis wishes he had his winter coat with him, or his favourite sweater, something more substantial to go outside in. He does not even have his gloves. He tightens the belt of his dressing gown.

Someone, thinks Lewis, is going to come into this house and pull out all the cupboards and appliances, tear up the tiles, strip the crazy wallpaper. They will put this old kitchen into a rusting yellow bin. They will want everything new. They will have to have the wiring done, he thinks.

Sydney opens the door, letting the dog out first.

Lewis, the last down the path, looks for broken windows or a bottle smashed on the ground, but there is nothing to see. He looks for a ticket on the windshield of the car, a clamp on the wheel, but there is nothing there, nothing to say that they have done anything wrong. There is no warden walking away from the car with the registration number in a notebook.

Lewis pauses before getting in. Putting his book down on the roof of the car, he checks his slippers, as if he might have mud on them, or horse shit, evidence that he has been here, closer to the heart of the countryside, closer to nature, than he has been in years. His slippers, though, illuminated beneath a street lamp, are very clean.

As they set off, Lewis says, 'Barry knows where I live.'

'Lock your door,' says Sydney. 'You'll be fine.'

Lewis imagines Barry sitting on his doorstep, waiting for him to come home, or rattling the front door in the middle of the night, and then the back door, trying the windows. He will have to remember to bolt the back door, to keep his windows locked. He will lie awake, listening.

He would rather not go home, but where else would he go? He cannot stay here—Sydney's house is also known to Barry Bolton, and, besides, it has been sold. At Ruth's house, he would have to sleep a partition wall away from Ruth and John's room. The house on Small Street no longer exists and he cannot sleep at the nursing home.

They drive back up the lane, the ground rough beneath their wheels, their lights shining through the darkness ahead, and Lewis thinks of the cargo ship that could not dock. He wants to always be here, in the yellow car, with Sydney.

'You're not the one who's got what Barry wants,' says Sydney. 'And when he comes looking for me, I'll be long gone.'

It is not much use, anyway, locking his doors and windows, when he will see Barry in the nursing home at teatime on Sunday. He pictures a showdown in the lavender-coloured living room, a heated confrontation with dolphin song in the background. Lewis will say that he does not have the car, that Sydney has it. Barry, standing a touch too close, will ask where Sydney is, and Lewis will say, quite honestly, that he does not know.

'You must have some money, though,' says Lewis. 'You must have made some money from your books. Why can't you just give Barry what you owe him?' If I had the money, thinks Lewis, I would buy a new suit and two shirts and a new coat, a new hat, new gloves, the lot.

'The money I've got,' says Sydney, 'is going to take me far away from here.'

Lewis is sitting on something hard. Reaching under his bottom, he extracts his spare pair of glasses. They are a bit bent but not broken. He puts them on, twisting round the rearview mirror to look at his face, clean-shaven but no longer smooth-skinned; at his shorn hair, his schoolboy cut, all the colour and thickness gone. He looks nothing like a schoolboy; he looks like the old man he is.

Even though he cannot see the back of his neck, the site of the mole's removal, he is aware of the growth having gone, and of feeling strangely bare. It feels sore. He thinks about Sydney's hand being there, about his dirty fingers, his being a bit rough. He feels as if the stitches—the stitch—might have been pulled through the edge of the wound, opening it up again. He imagines a small hole in his body, his insides showing. He will have to walk back to the surgery and it will make his knee hurt. When he gets home, he will go to the bathroom and inspect the wound using Edie's hand mirror. Perhaps he will find that the wound is fine and looks just as it did before.

He does not, he suddenly realises, have his book. He feels like Mr Benn going home without a souvenir in his pocket. He has no seashell, no wooden spoon.

'What will you do with the dog,' asks Lewis, 'while you're away?' He twists around to look at the elderly golden retriever smiling on the back seat of the car. 'I could have her,' he says. 'I could look after her.'

They speed down the long, dark country lane with their headlights on full beam and it makes Lewis think of flying, of what flying might be like, and of how you would be fine, you would be safe, up there in the air.

ACKNOWLEDGEMENTS

THANKS AS EVER to my first readers and trusted advisers: my supportive and eagle-eyed husband Dan and my furiously hardworking agent and editor Nick Royle. Thanks also to Arthur for being on my team. (The children in this story are fictional; Arthur is the best climber and explorer I know.) Thanks Jen and Chris Hamilton-Emery at Salt for their enthusiasm, and to Dan Wells and John Metcalf at Biblioasis for championing this novel in North America. Thanks to John Oakey for a beautiful cover in the UK, and to Gordon Robertson for an equally evocative North American cover. Thanks to my late father for responding to my enquiries about Billy Graham's visit to Manchester in 1961, to Annette for memories of seeing Billy Graham in London in the 1950s, and to Penny for proposing going to see Billy Graham in a tent in Loughborough in 1989. Thanks to the café at Manor Farm in East Leake—where a good deal of this novel was written while my son was at pre-school—for the coffee and a seat by the radiator in the New Year and the cold spring of 2013, and thanks to The Windmill in Wymeswold for having such a fine collection of curious old books.

The book about the physics of the future that Sydney mentions is *Physics of the Future: The Inventions That Will Transform Our Lives* by Michio Kaku, and the scientist 'talking about rubber bands' is Richard Feynman. 'We that are alive, that are left, shall . . . be caught up in the clouds, to meet the Lord in the air. Then we will be with the Lord forever' is from the New Testament (I. Thessalonians). 'The sky-lark and thrush, / The birds of the bush' is from 'The Ecchoing Green' by William Blake, and 'breathing English air, / Washed by the rivers, blest by suns of home' is from 'The Soldier' by Rupert Brooke. 'Pack up the stars, dismantle the sun' is a misquotation of W.H. Auden's 'Pack up the moon and dismantle the sun'. 'Have you ever tried jiu-jitsu?. . . I'll show you what I can, if you like' is from D.H. Lawrence's *Women in Love*, and 'great tufts of primroses under the hazels', 'dandelions making suns, the first daisies' and 'columbines and campions, and new-mown hay, and oak-tufts and honeysuckle' are from *Lady Chatterley's Lover*. 'Tonight is mine' is from Bram Stoker's *Dracula*.

ALISON MOORE's first novel, *The Lighthouse*, was short-listed for the Man Booker Prize 2012 and the National Book Awards 2012 (New Writer of the Year), winning the McKitterick Prize 2013. Her shorter fiction has been published in *Best British Short Stories* anthologies and in her debut collection *The Pre-War House and Other Stories*, whose title story won a novella prize. Born in Manchester in 1971, she lives near Nottingham with her husband Dan and son Arthur.

ELL THE WORLD
THIS BOOK WAS

Good	Bad	So so
✓		